Rachel M. Varble

THREE AGAINST LONDON

Illustrated by
C. WALTER HODGES

DOUBLEDAY & COMPANY, INC.
GARDEN CITY, NEW YORK

Library of Congress Catalog Card Number 62–11441
Copyright © 1962 by Rachel M. Varble
All Rights Reserved
Printed in the United States of America

THREE AGAINST
LONDON

A BOY CAN become a man in a short space of time if dire things happen, causing him to act. So it was with Amos Skeet, aged sixteen, of the Thames waterfront.

At first there was a muffled roar, the sound coming from a downstream direction; then lesser booms, almost velvety, as they died away. It was the good ship *London* blowing up, and Amos Skeet's father was a sailor aboard her.

Amos was slow and patient and handsome, a muscular youth, not through growing, with large hands and feet. He was carrying a keg of herring when the explosion came. Setting the keg on the cobbles of Gravesend, he scratched his elbows thoughtfully.

"It's gunpowder down at the ships," he announced to his companion, a younger boy. "Go wait at the dock while I deliver the fish. We must board a barge and go down."

The boy went running. He was Kip Skeet, Amos's twelve-year-old brother. He resembled Amos in coloring, having the same sun-bleached hair and sea-blue eyes, but his features were blunter.

Amos moved as quickly as his load permitted. He made the delivery to Dolphin Tavern and collected the three shillings due his mother, the sale of pickled fish being part of their livelihood. Returning to the dock, he saw that Kip had spoken them a place in a barge and was waving him aboard.

"Hurry, can't you?" Kip shouted. "We can ship free if we scrounge down!" He waved his arms like a boatswain.

Amos glared at him, too winded to do more, and clambered to the big cluttered barge. As usual, Kip expected a miracle of speed. He exhorted Amos showily as they got under way, advising him how to dispose of his feet and make himself useful with the freight.

The occupants of the barge—watermen, ships' carpenters, and the like—were talking of the thundering noises they had heard. "It was like the crack o' doom!" said a carpenter. "Aye, the crack o' doom with echoes!"

As the Thames widened, other boats put out from shore and dropped down with them. All were making for the Hope, that reach of water below Gravesend where part of the Navy was anchored.

At the Hope, nothing was learned. Sailors hung over ships' rails and swarmed the decks, shouting and demanding news. An acrid smoke was drifting overhead. Now and again came shouts of "Lea Roads!" and "Hither side of Nore buoy!"

"That be strange," said the bargemaster to a helper. "The Fleet be here and at Chatham. What's at Lea Roads, I ask ye?"

Amos and Kip crept close to listen, for the men who oared the barges, the veteran watermen, knew the river.

"They do say this," said the second, "old Lawson's bringin' up his flagship today from Chatham."

"The *London?*" Kip asked before Amos could find his voice.

"Aye, boy, the *London.* She's due for overhaul after Algiers."

"Our dad's a sailor on the *London,*" Amos said gravely to the watermen. "You can count on it, the old *London's* not in trouble."

"Aye, sure an' fer a fact." The two watermen exchanged uncertain glances and fell mum.

The crew rowed effectively, having agreed to go on. When they approached the mouth of Lea River they sought the left bank of the Thames, as other barges were doing, and put in there; and everybody went ashore, silent and gaping.

An unbelievable sight, nightmarish and grotesque, lay before them. The roundhouse of a ship protruded above the water, and some rowboats were tied to it, like water bugs around a lily pad. The boats were of every shape and condition, but the proud Navy must use them now. In the wherries huddled a score or more of persons who had been rescued from the sunken ship.

"She be the *London*," a sailor said with awe. "She blew apart, she did, and lays there covered, all but 'er eyebrows."

"The men on 'er!" Kip Skeet shouted, tugging at the sailor's sleeve. "Where's the rest of you?"

"Yes," Amos demanded, "where's the rest of you? Tell where!"

"I can't know where they be, boys. I'm ashore from the *St. George*." All watched as the boats above the submerged ship were rowed clear of her and brought to a wharf.

The crowd, the Skeet boys to the fore, ran along the quay to meet them and watched stolidly as the survivors were put ashore. They were mostly officers, only half a dozen men being in common jackets. Amos and Kip looked at them avidly. None was seaman Tom Skeet. "Where's our dad?" Kip called. He shouted it until Amos laid a hand over his mouth and silenced him.

"There's a boat yet to come," someone said. "More's expected."

But out of the roundhouse at last crawled only one man to enter the wherry. The sun shone on the glittering braid of his drenched uniform. He was Sir John Lawson, Vice-Admiral of the Fleet, who had been searching for the last of his survivors. He came alone, rowed by four fishermen, and stepped ashore grimly. He had lost more than three hundred men and officers, some of them his kinsmen.

To this man, Kip Skeet ran wildly. "Where's our dad, sir? We want to know where our dad is! Here's my brother and me, come to help. Remember the name Tom Skeet, sir?"

Vice-Admiral Lawson looked at the boys in pain and bewilderment. His jaw tightened. "Dead," he said. "Drowned, if he was aboard. Let me pass."

The boys drew aside, stood for a while in the fringe of the

crowd. As usual, Kip spoke first. "Notice what he said, Amos— *if he was aboard*. Maybe he stayed behind at Chatham."

"Yes, Kip, it could be. It just might be."

But from a rescued sailor they heard the news they dreaded. The man was called Yar, because he came from Yarmouth, and the boys knew him by sight. When they asked him if he knew anything of their father, he told them he had seen Tom Skeet on deck a while before the explosion. "He was splicin' a rope. That's all I remember now," he said regretfully. "I must away home."

Though bereft of hope now, Amos and Kip stayed on. Once, as a reckless prank, they had stolen aboard the *London* at Chatham, with a boy named Toby Wayneman. All the officers and most of the crew were ashore. With only the stars to light them, they had trod the *London's* famous planks and looked up at her great masts. The remembrance of her beauty was still with them. Amos felt a sudden pride that their dad should have so fine a coffin, and he wanted to tell Kip, but he could not put it into words.

They listened to the talk as people came and went. Eighty pieces of brass, folk said, think of it! Eighty brass cannon that ought to be salvaged. But, oh, the lives that could never be salvaged! . . . Women came, seeking their men, some of them leading little children, all of them moaning in grief or rebellion.

Toward evening there appeared on the wharf a very elderly priest of the Established Church, a follower of the old Roman ways. He pled with the wherrymen, first one, then another, to take him to the stricken ship. Finally he was rowed out to the listing roundhouse and fearlessly entered it, to say his prayers for the souls of those lying below.

When he returned to the shore, Kip, made talkative by grief, detained him. "Our dad was a sailor on the *London*," he said in a rush. "Tom Skeet was his name. He was about to be forty years old. I'm Kip Skeet. This here's my brother, Amos."

"God pity you. What will your mother do?"

"She'll cure herring, like always, and drink rum."

Again Amos laid his hand over his brother's mouth.

The old priest turned his eyes to the Thames. "What was your father's faith?" he inquired. "What is the family way?"

"Our dad says we are Puritans, is all I know," replied Amos.

"Have you ever been baptized?"

"No, we've ne'er been," Amos said.

"Tut, tut," the old clergyman made answer. "Would you object to my doing that for you?"

"I wouldn't mind," Amos said politely. "Would you mind, Kip?"

Kip said it would be all right with him. Hearing which, the decrepit one fetched up some water from Lea River in a shell and extended a proud hand. "Your father's name of Thomas I add to both your names," he said. "Wear it well." He quickly sprinkled them and made the sign of the Cross on their foreheads, saying his ancient formal words. "That can never hurt you," he explained. He smiled absently, added, "Ho, Oliver Cromwell, I'd have done the same for you!" Then he went away.

Amos and Kip stayed the night at Lea Roads, as many others did. When they became tired past endurance they crawled into a pile of tattered sailcloth and fell asleep to the tolling of Nore buoy.

Next day, the city of London mourned the loss of its namesake, right grimly. At the Royal Exchange, merchants and guilds began to raise a subscription to replace her, as a gift to King Charles, for nothing comforted the Merry Monarch like a purse. As much as his faithful subjects tried to idealize him, they knew this to be a fact: Charles would rather lose ten old worn-out sailors than ten newly minted guineas.

Bells tolled. Heads were shaken gravely at how this loss would embolden the Dutch. But at Wapping and Blackwall, and along the docks of Deptford and Greenwich, the regret was for the sailors who would never come home again to this waterfront.

Yar, the sailor who had seen Tom Skeet before the sinking,

went home to Wapping, where his wife awaited him. Though bruised and battered, he was miraculously alive. Even a little tin of tea he had brought his wife was intact. After she had ministered to him with arnica and cries of joy, he remembered the Skeet boys, and told her how they had questioned him.

"I 'ad naught but ill news for 'em," he said. "They looked bedazed. They mayn't come 'ome for a while. Go to Dick's Shore and tell Skeet's widow what's 'appened. They live in a boat alongside the Nokes fish sheds."

Yar's wife went reluctantly on her sad mission. She had no acquaintance with Mrs. Skeet, but a sailor's wife is the one to apprise a sailor's wife when the blow falls.

Though Mrs. Skeet was not well known, being born and raised a country girl, and never having understood Cockney ways, folk rallied to her when the news got around. The shanty boat took on the dignity that death always lends a dwelling. Someone tied a streamer of crepe to the door latch. Others brought food, such as they could spare. Yar's wife shared the very tea that had come from a far place in her husband's pocket.

When the newly made widow was alone at last, she began to sound the depths of her loss. Tom Skeet would never again fill this place with his cheerful presence when a voyage ended. Would no more lay his uncertain pay on the deal table. Would not again embrace her and warn her against rum, or tousle the heads of his boys and cuff them for wrongdoing.

The boys! They were long overdue. Yar had talked to them at Lea Roads; they knew their father had perished. Why, then, did they not come home?

As Mrs. Skeet stood on the houseboat's deck, scanning the river, there emerged from the landward mist a flashily dressed man of middle age and middle size. He would have been handsome but for his shifty expression. He was called Shark, either because of his pointed teeth or his predatory ways. This man was a trader of the lowest order, buying for drink or a few coins the very keepsakes the sailors were bringing to their wives.

Before the poor women could clap eyes on their gifts, Shark often had them. Once he managed to get a valuable piece of ambergris from Tom Skeet because the Navy lagged in paying off Tom's ship. Another time, he plied a weak-willed sailor with gin in a tavern and gave him sixpence for a bag of spice —as ugly a piece of robbery as was ever executed without knife or pistol, for the sailor had an ailing child in need of medicine.

This Shark, this rogue without known name or title, had lodgings in a mean street in Whitechapel. But he desired a spot on the water. As he passed through the Limehouse area on his shady enterprises he always gazed at Tom Skeet's boat. He now boarded the marine shanty and addressed Mrs. Skeet in an oily voice. "I've 'eard the news," he said. "It fair rips my 'eart out. Ye'll be in need o' some money, likely. I can advance ye a loan, Mistress Skeet, if ye'll sell me Tom Skeet's land boots and 'is clothes and fowlin' piece. Sell 'em cheap, that is."

Mrs. Skeet uttered a cry of angry protest. "I'll not sell ye a thing my dear one e'er wore, nor aught he handled! My own boys will want the little he had. Be off!"

"Ye're upset," the scavenger said. "Ye're beside yoursel' with grief. Ye don't know which way to turn. Where's yer lads now, by the way? Slitherin' out o' the fish trade? Leavin' ye to carry on by yoursel'? Run off a'ready?"

"No, no," Mrs. Skeet moaned. "Surely not! They went down to Gravesend yesterday to take a keg o' fish to the Dolphin. The Dolphin's a steady customer o' ours."

"Then Dolphin pays regular. No doubt Dolphin paid yer boys yestiddy when the keg was set down. Would ye know the exact sum? Would it be enough, say, to tempt a pair o' wild lads to go to Chatham on a frolic?"

"They've ne'er been wild," Mrs. Skeet replied, but her sad fears mounted, and she wept. Shark made clucking sounds of sympathy. He took a green glass bottle from an inner pocket of his coat and held it in his hands, carelessly studying its square shape, its pretty stopper. He knew poor Mrs. Skeet's weakness. Though she never mingled with roistering men and women in tap rooms or in the streets, she did drink in solitude —for loneliness, folk said—and there would be days at a time when she wore her dresses wrong side out, and neglected to cook the meals, and failed to pickle the fish she was pledged to sell. It was well known at Nokes' fish shed, where she obtained her herring, but it was not spoken of openly. She was Tom Skeet's faithful wife, and such was her status, whether he was near or absent. Though shrill and given to maudlin self-reproach, Mrs. Skeet was not profane or lewd. Once she had been comely, and some traces of her country beauty still lingered. But her uncombed hair and smudged face marked her as a derelict, bereft of a vanity that might have saved her. Amos and Kip were ashamed of her, and that was the sad truth, though they loved her loyally.

Shark took her by the elbow and set her on an upturned brine tub. "Poor Mistress Skeet," he said, " 'ave a little nip o' this rum to warm yer bones. Ye're a woman that wants lookin' after."

Mrs. Skeet sighed. She had grown up in her father's tavern at Brentwood, a respectable wayside house, and while she was yet a child with yellow curls and a blue ribbon, folk would set her on the bar and give her sips of this and that to hear her chatter. Ale in summer when the bees were on the blossoms, sack posset when the evenings were frosty, mulled rum on a wet March day like this. Yes, Jamaican rum most of all; for her father owned kegs of it that he had bought as contraband off a ship that sank in Blackwater Bay. When Tom Skeet married her and took her to live in London, he had no idea that rum was in the marrow of her young bones.

"I'll have no part of your bottle, Shark," Mrs. Skeet said now. "Many's the time my Tom warned me against booze-rum. This day forward, I'll be foregoin' the stuff, for the boys' sake."

"Make yer widowhood bleak, must ye? Deprive yersel' o' every comfort? That's not English, 'ardly. By the way, Widow Skeet, will ye apply fer aid from the Ancient Fishmongers' Company?"

Mrs. Skeet gave the man a quick and wary look. "Not hardly."

"Do ye mean ye're not known to that guild, ma'am?"

"Tom Skeet was a seaman, I'll have ye remember. What had he to do with a City company?"

"I reckon 'e knew 'is wife an' boys 'awked fish. Did he ne'er buy you a license at Fishmongers' Hall?"

Mrs. Skeet retorted truthfully, "Tom ne'er did, no. But then, we've ne'er had a stall, and we don't cry our wares, neither. We don't go near Billingsgate to vie with folk there. We sell mostly downriver, that we do. Places like Greenwich and Woolwich and Gravesend."

"But last week I seen yer lads carryin' a firkin o' fish to Navy Yard, Mistress Skeet. I watched 'em enter. That be inside the City, unless the Wall's moved?"

"We've got a buyer in Navy Yard; I admit to it. A man named Pepys. He takes from us regular. He likes our herrin' because I put 'em down with herbs. Yes, herbs goes into the brine. That's a rule I learned in childhood. It's a chore to do, and I'm obliged to charge a little more, but Pepys pays."

"Mr. Sam'l Pepys, eh?" Shark narrowed his eyes. "There's three or four ways to say that name, but it's all one man. 'E's clerk fer the Admiralty. 'As to do with payin' seamen, too. Puts 'is finger in a lot o' pies. Does 'e know 'e's buyin' fish from unlicensed folk?"

"Amos and Kip ne'er have words with Mr. Pepys. They deal with Mrs. Pepys and a young girl that works there, Sue Stokes."

"Yer boys could be put in jail fer this, Widow Skeet, should anybody take it in 'is 'ead to report it. Or they could be shipped to Barbados if the judges at Old Bailey was 'avin' a bad day."

"Oh, woe's me! surely not!" The poor soul began to weep again, the threat of danger compounding her sorrow. To be called "Widow Skeet" unnerved her, too. Twilight was falling; a March mist was closing in, dismal and raw.

"Master Shark," she sobbed, "I'd thank ye not to mention our carryin' fish to Navy Yard, that I would."

"I can forget it, Widow Skeet, if ye can see yer way clear to 'andin' over those articles I want. Will ye drink to a sharp bargain 'twixt two chums?"

"Don't call us chums!" Mrs. Skeet moaned, her native decency outraged; but she eyed the bottle longingly.

Suddenly a tall blond youth came aboard, closely followed by a panting younger lad, and Mrs. Skeet saw that her sons had come home. "Oh, my poor fatherless boys," she cried, "it's ye, both!"

"Of course, Muvver," Amos answered, using the pronunciation of the London lanes. He made an effort to speak matter-of-factly, for he saw that their mother was in a bad way. "Kip and me stayed by the ship, Muvver. It was the only way we could give him burial. We stayed till the roundhouse broke apart and sank." Then he saw Shark and exclaimed, "What's that man doing here?"

"Yes," Kip said, stepping forward to stand beside his brother. "What does he want of us? What's old Shark after?"

"Your dad's land boots and clothes and fowlin' piece. I'm about to fetch 'em for him. We've made a pact, Shark and me."

"Blimey!" Amos exclaimed. He looked at the green bottle in Shark's hand and sensed that it was being offered his poor weak mother to deprive them of Tom Skeet's personal belongings. His blood pounded in his ears. "Get away from here," he shouted, "and ne'er come back!"

"Not so fast, me fine young chaps," Shark retorted in a cool way. "Them that 'awks fish without a license takes a risk. And them that goes to Navy Yard to do it is bold beyond common. The Widow Skeet, 'ere, is afraid I'll make a tale of it."

"You're double trouble to us with your bottle and your tattlin'," Amos said hotly. "Leave off botherin' my mother, or I'll knock you to Dover! Go ashore!"

"When it suits me, sprout." Shark turned his ugly attention to Kip, who shrank a little. "An' what 'ave we got 'ere? Another 'alf-cured bloater?"

Amos lunged and struck with all his strength. The man

went overboard grotesquely, the bottle preceding him, his arms outspread, his face wearing a look of furious surprise. From the fish shed came a cackle of laughter. That and a splash were all. There was no sound of a man saving himself.

"What have ye done, Amos?" Mrs. Skeet asked shrilly.

The three of them went to the boat's edge and peered at the darkening water, willing a hateful head to appear, willing a hateful hand to grasp their timbers or the dock. Nothing met their eyes but the natural movements of the great river. Amos removed his coat, kicked off his shoes, and dived. Kip went ashore and ran along the bank, downstream, as the current went. Mrs. Skeet shouted for help incoherently.

Mr. Nokes, the man who owned the aquatic market alongside, emerged onto his dock and spoke to his old fish cleaner. "What goes on at the Skeets'? Is the poor woman boozy because Tom's dead and gone?"

"No, she ain't, master. She be in 'er right mind." He rested his knife and peered at the river, scanning one of Lime House's darker reaches. "'Er boy, Amos, knocked Shark o'erboard, an' the Shark be drowned, plum drowned."

"Drowned, you say! Couldn't Shark swim?"

"It 'pears like he couldn't. Good riddance!" Again the dock drudge laughed eerily; he loathed and rejected Shark more than the entrails he threw into the Thames. The old man's strange mumblings mingled with Mrs. Skeet's laments while Mr. Nokes put on his coat to go home. Nokes had always kept to business with his shiftless neighbors, as he called them. He was several cuts above them, socially, and he owned a house in Stepney. Tonight his gait was faster than usual as he went home to that house.

Downriver, Amos swam wearily to shore, led by his brother's guiding calls in an area without docks. Climbing the sludgy bank, he lay there, confused and disheartened. He could hear Kip near at hand, could see a stumbling woman with a lantern coming toward him. Her cries of distress identified her as his mother.

" 'Twas no good, Kip," he panted, "ebb got 'im."

When Mrs. Skeet found her sons, her noise abated. But she had aroused some prowlers, and several of these unknown persons now materialized from the twilight of the docks. As always, she was articulate. "My boy here, Amos Skeet, dived in the river to lift a man from drowning, but he's not found man or body." Then she added—unnecessarily, it seemed to Amos and Kip—"It was a man he'd shoved off our boat."

Heavy silence met this announcement, and Mrs. Skeet added details. "He was a rascal known as Shark, a sporty chap with pointed teeth and curly hair. He had a rovin' eye, and he was always dressed to the gills. He'd cut the buttons off your coat if ye didn't look sharp."

"The Shark, did she say?" There was some mumbling among the men, then muted laughter.

"It's not a thing to snicker at," Mrs. Skeet said bravely, "and shame on them that laughs at a graveside! My Amos here didn't mean it to end so. Did ye, Amos?"

"No," answered Amos, retching salt water. He got up shakily and took the lantern from his mother's hand and gave it to Kip. "Lead her home," he said, "before she talks her head off."

A thin, bearded man in a cape and slouch hat stepped out of the dark and touched Amos on the shoulder. That he was a common footpad was evident. "Hark ye, cove," he said, "I've set at cards with Shark many's the time. Gleek's our game. The boldest wins."

"So?" Amos answered, puzzled and impatient.

"The Shark's drowned or not drowned as ye want to look at it, cove. Somebody climbed aboard a wherry out there not a minute agone, midstream. First I thought 'twere a waterman that had swum after a piece o' plunder. Now I ain't sure. It's the way Shark would play it."

"Thank you," Amos said. "Thank you a-plenty!"

He followed Kip's lantern home, careful not to tread on his mother's bedraggled black skirt—her best dress, put on that morning in honor of Tom Skeet, the good sailor.

Susan Stokes, the little brunette 'prentice cook at the house of Mr. and Mrs. Samuel Pepys, was in love with Amos. She was a rosy-cheeked, clear-eyed girl with glossy dark hair that she persistently kept in control. In this struggle with her hair, Susan brushed it away from her forehead and ears and neck, tying it on top of her head with a ribbon and letting the short ends form a bird's nest. It was not stylish: it looked as if she were waiting for a hairdresser to add bangs or a chignon.

She was almost pretty, and growing more so, though no one noticed. She was more daintily clean than a kitchen maid was expected to be. There was a sweet, fresh smell about her, because she sprinkled dried lavender through her coarse little dresses and shifts when she washed them and put them away.

Though Susan was barely fifteen, her love for Amos Skeet was intense; she trembled and blushed at the sight of him. Amos was not aware of this. He found her agreeable. He thought her pretty enough in a dark-eyed, curly topped way, but he never saw such a girl for dropping things and bumping into you.

"Oh, forgive me!" she would exclaim in an agonized voice when she had been especially gauche. "I don't know what's got into me today!"

"Don't mention it," he would reply, puzzled.

Susan would lower her eyes before Amos's steady blue gaze and would fix her attention on his large shapely hands, as if expecting him to perform a piece of magic—extract a pearl from a fish's mouth, or snap his fingers and pluck a full-blown rose from the air. But she always offered him a cup of chocolate or a bowl of soup from the back of the stove and talked to him while he consumed it. At these times, she was at ease.

Susan knew little about the Skeet family except that Amos and Kip and their mother lived downriver from the Tower of London, and that they conducted a salt-herring business while Mr. Skeet was at sea. At first she had been startled by the boys' Cockney way of speaking. But as her infatuation for

Amos grew, it seemed to matter less. Besides, she noticed that his grammar was improving; and there came the day when he said to her, "If I make a bad error in my speech, kindly correct me." She dared to do this, and no bones were broken. As for Kip, he continued to speak as he pleased, though Amos would nudge him if he slouched or forgot to take off his cap.

When Susan heard Mr. and Mrs. Pepys talk of the sinking of the *London,* she failed to connect the tragedy with her adored. She did not dwell on it, for it was a calamity beyond her comprehension. In the Pepys kitchen there was trouble enough at the moment. Besse the cook, a woman on whom Susan depended, had just quit the house with hot words, Besse storming, Mrs. Pepys weeping, and Susan found herself in charge of a dirty kitchen. A new servant arrived, but she was a chambermaid, a haughty woman who refused to lend a hand at the cookstove.

Another thing upset Susan. Three fashionable young ladies from the country, the Montagu sisters, often came to London for a visit at their father's town house; then they would drop in at the Pepys abode whenever it suited them, for Mr. Pepys was their cousin. Their father, Sir Edward, was covered with titles: Earl of Sandwich, Viscount Hinchingbroke, Baron of St. Noet's, Knight of the Garter, Master of the Wardrobe, and sometime Admiral of the Fleet. Mr. Pepys owed his job as a clerk in the Admiralty to him, and when any of the young Montagus came to Navy Yard, nothing was too much trouble. My lord's four sons and three daughters had only to state their wishes, and every one jumped.

Jemimah Montagu was engaged to be married; Paulina was frail and peevish; those two hardly counted in Susan Stokes' life except to cause more work. But Anne was different. Lively, blonde, tall, graceful, she was a girl who appreciated the opposite sex, even a sunburned delivery boy who was speechless at the sight of her. More than once she had questioned Susan about "that boy Amos" and she pretended to have a great taste for salt herring.

One night Susan prayed tiredly before getting into bed. "Dear Lord, don't let Lady Anne float over me that way. Take her back to the country, dear Lord, and keep her there!"

Susan knew this supplication to be out of line, for she had a prayer book. She and her widowed mother used to live with her grandfather, a retired barrister, a graduate of Gray's Inn, who resided in Chancery Lane. He had taught Susan to read and write. When the old gentleman died, innocently depriving them of shelter, Mrs. Stokes solved her problem by marrying the personable sexton of St. Bride's Church—beneath her in birth and breeding—and moving into his quarters. In due time there arrived two offspring of this union to tax the sleeping quarters and the larder. One day the harried sexton took his stepchild aside and requested her to find employment and move out.

"Let your mother think it's your own idea," he said. "You're useful with the young ones, but I can't afford to keep you."

Susan's fourteen-year-old heart was hurt and offended. She went for a walk up Shoe Lane to pull herself together. Returning, she told her mother she wanted to hire out as a housemaid.

"Not while you're so young, Sue!" her mother protested.

"Yes, right away. I want to earn money for some new clothes."

Susan found a job because another girl defaulted. Jennie, a wild parish charge, had gone to work for young Mr. and Mrs. Samuel Pepys in Navy Yard, stayed long enough to get a new outfit of clothes, and ran away next day while going to the bakeshop. Pepys went angrily to St. Bride's beadle—a sort of truant officer—and ordered him to get the clothes from Jennie and send him another prospect, a girl the clothes would fit. The beadle told the sexton, the sexton recommended his stepdaughter, Susan Stokes.

But Susan's mother said she must know something about these Pepys people before she'd permit her daughter to go off and work for them. Who were they?

It turned out that Samuel Pepys was a brother of Mr. Tom Pepys, a tailor of St. Bride's parish. Their father too had been a tailor but had inherited a little estate and moved to the country. Tom Pepys assured Susan's mother that the girl would be in an interesting place. "My brother and his wife are high-tempered," the tailor said, "but gay as larks. It's never dull there."

"High-tempered and gay," mused Susan's mother with mis-givings.

"But decent, ma'am. They've got a pew in St. Olave's Church."

And so Susan went to work there on August 21, 1663, as is stated in Mr. Pepys' famous diary. Thereafter, everything Pepys recorded of her was complimentary, though once he called her a cheap name, perhaps because it was easily put into his shorthand:

Spent all the morning drawing up a letter to Mr. Coventry about preserving of masts. To my uncle's to supper. So home to prayers and to bed. My wife called up the people to washing by four o'clock in the morning; and our little girle Susan is a most admirable slut and pleases us mightily, doing more service than both the others and deserves wages better.

Pepys' diary was his secret. He kept it locked away in Navy Office and wrote in it for the pleasure it would bring to him in future years. It told of great events in which he played a decisive part. It also recorded his mean acts and his vanity. In it, he tagged people against his own forgetfulness. He al-ways wrote Susan Stokes into the record as "little Sue" or "little Susan," because he had formerly employed a thieving older woman named Susan.

It was only when Amos Skeet was in sight that "little Sue" lost her tongue and her poise. Usually she was serene enough. She could make decisions and assert herself. Her em-ployers liked her self-reliance, for they were the greatest gad-abouts in London and often forgot to plan the meals. They would invite guests to dinner on impulse. Susan would wade into these difficulties with a shrug and a laugh, inducing the other servants to follow. It was very unfair, then, that when she went a step too far in getting the work done, she was cruelly punished for it. There was a Scotswoman, a sailor's wife, who had not seen her husband in two years and believed him lost at sea. She wanted news of him and needed his pay, so day after day she would come to Navy Office and ask for audience with the commissioners. Susan and Besse, in pity, often gave her food to take home to her children, and the poor creature was so grateful that she offered to help with the char work and washing. The arrangement was beneficial to all, but one day it ended badly, as Mr. Pepys' diary reveals:

Feb. 19th. Lay in bed, it being Lord's day, all the morning talking with my wife, sometimes pleased, sometimes displeased, and then up and to dinner. In the evening comes Mr. Andrews, and we sung together, and at supper hearing by accident of my mayds their letting in a roguing Scotch woman that haunts the office, to helpe them to washe and scoure in our house, and that very lately, I fell mightily out, and made my wife, to the disturbance of the house and neighbors, to beat our little girle, and then we shut her down into the cellar, and there she lay all night.

This happened shortly before the *London* sank, and it had a good deal to do with Besse's quitting the house in anger. Besse advised Susan to leave, but Susan could not act so rashly. Jobs for young persons were scarce, and she was too proud to return to the sexton's crowded little house and ask for keep.

Fortunately for all concerned, Mr. and Mrs. Pepys presently repented of their harshness. Mrs. Pepys said Susan need never again go to the cellar after dark, not even to fetch something.

"Were you frightened of the mice, you poor girl?" she asked contritely.

"The mice didn't bother me much," Sue replied guardedly.

Actually, Besse had taken her a lighted lantern and a little terrier, their neighbor Admiral Penn's own ratter, to make the night bearable. But the remembered pain and humiliation of the beating, Mrs. Pepys having struck her about the arms and shoulders any which way with her belt, moved her to protest. "Never try to beat me again, Mrs. Pepys, if you please. I'm not used to it."

"No? I used to be boxed right often when I was young," Mrs. Pepys confided. "Sam got whipped, too. That's why we're not queasy about hitting our servants. We used to have a page, a red-haired boy named Wayneman, that was always getting into trouble. Sam wore out a dried eel or two, whipping that boy."

"What became of him, Mrs. Pepys?" Susan asked.

"He ran away, nobody knows where."

"There you are!" Susan replied in a peppery way. "He ran off and lost himself because he couldn't stand being so—"

She could not think of the word *degraded*, so she sighed and went to the scullery to get fuel to replenish the fire. Suddenly she knew she could not quit this house and sever herself from its people as Wayneman had done, for she might nevermore see Amos Skeet if she did. She had no contact with Amos except in this kitchen.

Thinking of him now, she laid kindling and coals on the grate of the stove and fanned it to flame. Soon the room was warm and glowing, and so was her heart.

When the Skeet family returned to the shanty boat after Shark's disappearance, they took counsel together. Amos sat hunched on his bunk, wrapped in his one blanket, trying to think what had happened and to interpret it to his mother and Kip.

"I told Shark to leave, but he wouldn't. Then I hit him without notice. He looked like a spread eagle in the air. After the splash I ne'er heard a sound from him. When I dived I felt around where he ought to be. I swum and groped till I gave out."

"We must tell somebody!" Mrs. Skeet wailed.

"You've already done that," Kip reminded her.

"She means we ought to make a report to somebody," Amos said. "But to who, I ask you?"

"There's magistrates," Mrs. Skeet pointed out. "Don't they listen and write things down? I believe a magistrate would write down for you, 'I, Amos Skeet, ne'er meant to drown the man.'"

"Wait there," Amos said, "I'm not sure Shark's dead. You heard what that chap said; he saw somebody clamber in a boat, midstream. That's the way Shark would play it, he said."

"Why would he?" Kip asked. "Why would a man want to act drowned when he wasn't?"

"I don't know," Amos answered wearily. He ached from head to feet, and his throat hurt most of all. He had become chilled when sleeping in the open at Lea Roads. Grief for his father, the need to bolster Kip, the dread of facing his mother—these things had further depleted him. And now that he had reached home, nightmarish episodes continued to occur. There was a longing and a need inside him to stop struggling for a while. "I must give way," he mumbled, for he knew he was very ill. He collapsed.

"Look!" Kip shouted to his mother. "Amos has fell in a fit!"

It did appear to be a seizure, but it was a natural one. Amos had been taken with a chill and could not control his jerking muscles and chattering teeth.

They put him prone on his bed and covered him with an extra blanket. Mrs. Skeet made a hot drink of China tea and ginger, and forced him to gulp it. She was proud that she had both of these restoratives in the house. Afterward she dosed Kip and herself and induced Kip to go to bed. For the first time in years she was efficient. As she sat on a stool with her back against the timbers, keeping watch over her sick son, the sorrow of her new widowhood was diminished somewhat, and her moral resolves were strengthened.

Amos wakened in a fever. He lay ill for a fortnight. At times he was out of his head and inclined to shout. But he was a strong boy with no intention of dying, and eventually he was able to get to his feet and walk about the room with his hand on Kip's shoulder. He knew there were things to be done, and he was impatient to get at them. He must collect his father's pay and must hold out against taking "tickets" instead of money, for that was a tricky game the commissioners had, and you must beat them at it. And, too, he must find steady work.

Kip, for his part, had risen to the family need while Amos lay ill. He had helped his mother pickle several kegs of herring and, on his own initiative, had sold the fish in small quantities in Stepney and Bethnal Green, hamlets that lay nearby. He bragged of his success one day when Amos seemed better.

"Did you hawk the fish?" Amos asked quickly. "Did you forget yourself and cry your wares?"

"Maybe I did a little," Kip admitted. "How else would people know I had 'em?"

"You ought not have done that!" Amos stormed. Though his legs were still weak, his temper and his voice were not. "You don't seem to have the sense of a calf!"

Mrs. Skeet intervened. "How else could we have got along, Amos? Kip's a clever boy. He's brought home enough to feed us beef brawn, and Scotty oats with sweetenin'."

Amos scowled and turned brusquely away. His mother and Kip knew the dangers of hawking without license. Why would they chance it? Then he realized it had been for his sake, of course. He could not have stomached brinish herring and hard ship's biscuit while he was weak and nauseated.

Seeing that Kip looked crestfallen, Amos went to him and threw an arm around his shoulder. "I ask your pardon, Kip, for bellowin' at you," he said. "You've done well, mighty well. But it was chancy."

"Let's get a hawker's license, Amos," Kip said. "I could shout all the way to Westminster, then."

"It would mean a layout of money at Fishmongers' Hall, Kip, and we'd be 'prenticed to whoever would take us. We'd likely have different masters and be lodged miles apart. We'd wear dirty leather aprons, and we'd gut fish all day. After that we'd sell fish for our masters, not for ourselves. No, thank you! That's not a life I'd choose for us. Dad always told us to try to better ourselves and to pick up a little learning. 'Don't follow the sea,' was another thing he said, 'because the sea's a dog's life with uncertain pay.' "

"So we can't be sailors, Amos?" Kip went and looked at the river. "Most boys follow after their fathers."

"I'd be willing to try it a while, Kip, but for one thing. Dad said we should stick together. You're too young to go to sea, and I'd not leave you to rat around the docks. Our mother couldn't handle you. Nor you couldn't handle her, for that matter. We've got to think of some proper work we can do hereabouts. Meantime we'll sell our herring downriver at the taverns, and I'll load carts at Victualing Yard whenever they'll hire me."

Mrs. Skeet, who had been listening, nodded agreement. She had never known how to make decisions. Before her husband went out with the Fleet, he would always instruct her in what to do: how to care for herself and the boys, how to keep the boat as a decent home. "Mr. Nokes will ne'er bother you," she remembered his saying, "if you and the lads don't bother Nokes. See that you don't. Buy fresh, cleaned herring from Nokes, a few at a time, and pay 'im prompt. Have the boys aid you in the pickling. Do it on deck, not indoors to smell up the quarters. Have the lads sell outside the City. Ne'er let 'em tangle with Billingsgate, nor with Queen's Market either."

It comforted Mrs. Skeet now to hear her older son up-holding his father's policies, if so those humble rules could be called; and she was elated to learn that Amos had no hankering to be a sailor, for he was almost ripe for it in age and size.

Amos sat on the shanty boat's deck for a few days in the bright spring sunshine, and every so often he would get to his feet and leap to the fishing shed to help the workers heave a cask or pull in a net. This brought the life back to his muscles. He was eager to be himself again, the strongest boy at Dick's Shore. One day he and Kip walked all over the Lime House area, and when they came to the old Lime House that had given the locality its name, they loitered. They had often played there as little boys. It was a row of great kilns where limestone and shells were converted to quicklime. Near it was the fine old timbered dwelling of Captain Marsh, whose ancestors had owned the lime works for more than two hundred years.

Captain Marsh was in his garden, espaliering a young pear tree, and he greeted the boys absent-mindedly. He was a retired sea captain of vast experience who often gave advice to the naval bigwigs. This year he was advising them to build royal fishing buses for revenue.

When he noticed that Amos and Kip kept watching him, he tried to be civil. "Used to see you boys around here when you were little tads. You've got a funny name—Skeet. It's of Dutch origin. Nothing to be ashamed of, Dutch blood. They make the best sailors."

"Our grandfather came from Holland," Amos said. "His name was Kip Skeet, the same as my brother here. He married an English woman and lived at Folkestone. They had a boy named Thomas who ran away to sea. That was our father. But he's dead now. Was on the *London*."

Captain Marsh straightened up. "Egad! Sorry to hear it! But that's the Navy for you. Danger, exhilaration, maybe a heroic death if you stay with it. Sit on that sea chest, boys, and I'll have some food brought out."

"You needn't, sir," said Amos stiffly, "we've eat today."

"Then eat again. Victuals are plentiful." He rang a bell, and an elderly female servant came out in response to its jangle. "Bring a pitcher of milk and some of those plum tarts," he told the woman. She did so, and the boys consumed all the tarts and several mugs of milk in a short time. But when

Captain Marsh rather bluntly offered Amos a handful of coins, he backed away.

"We didn't come begging, sir," he said in his plain, ungracious way. "We'll be off now, unless there's some yard work we could do for you? We're willing."

"There's no work. I've got a bunch of ailing sailors who hang around, and I employ 'em when I can." He studied Amos. "Why don't you go to sea, like your father did?"

"There's reasons I can't, sir," Amos said. "A good day to you."

As they left the premises they saw a public coach draw up at the gate; two men got out of it. One of them was Admiral Sir William Penn—a man everybody knew by sight—in a worn-out uniform.

"Who's the other one?" Kip asked in a low voice. Penn's companion was a rather young civilian with prominent blue eyes that seemed to see everything. He walked with a swing.

"It's Mr. Samuel Pepys," Amos mumbled, looking straight ahead, "the one Susan works for."

"Will we ever make another delivery there?" Kip asked. He was thinking of Susan's generous habit of handing out food.

Amos did not answer at once. He stopped and scratched his elbows. Then he declared, "Yes, we will, Kip. One more delivery anyway. We'll risk it."

He felt a desire to corner Susan and recite his troubles. He had a great need to tell her all the things that had happened to him since he had seen her last, even that ugly piece of business about Shark.

Kip prodded him. "I know why you want to go to Navy Yard again, Amos. You're taken with Susan Stokes. I can tell you love 'er. Come on, Amos, and say how much."

"I don't know what you mean, Kip. You can't *measure* the way you feel toward a girl, like with a pair of scales or a rule. But I hone to see Susan again, that's a fact." Another memory flashed, taking him unaware, dimming Susan; he'd not mind having another look at that beauty from the country who sometimes visited there. She had fluttered her eyelashes at him. She was sort of brazen. Would she slap him if he touched her cheek, or would she laugh? The uncertainty excited him. But it was not the sort of thing he could discuss with a boy four years younger than himself.

"We'd better get home and scrub the deck," he told Kip in a practical voice. "The old boat looks all right when she's clean." This was faint praise, for the houseboat was built of excellent timbers, stoutly joined. Tom Skeet had got her at a bargain in his youth. He had never ceased to be proud of his floating home, even at her weathered worst.

"Yesterday," Kip said, "some people in a sloop veered in close to us, and they looked at the letters on the side of our boat and laughed. Why did they?"

"Laughed, did they?" Amos said thoughtfully. Then his face reddened. "I'll tell you why they laughed, Kip. Our boat's name used to have ten letters in it. The way our dad painted it on was ENTERPRIZE—spelled wrong, I think. At least I once heard somebody say so. But the first half of the name's been banged off. What's left is PRIZE, like it was a rich sea haul, taken by the Navy. I'll buy a little paint in Wapping and put the letters back. And I'll ask Susan how's the best way to spell the word."

"Yeah. Let's not be laughed at."

"There's a Scot at the limekilns who's educated, Mr. Hugh McTarvish. He's offered to teach me a little arithmetic, so I won't be cheated in business. He might teach me to read and write, too, if I could find the time."

"I might ask his help, myself," Kip said. "I'm quicker than you are, Amos." The boy spoke the truth, and Amos forgave him.

Mrs. Skeet waved to them from the boat, still neat, still herself, as befitted the new leaf she had turned over.

The following day Amos resolved to see Susan.

He bathed and dressed himself in his best shirt and breeches and put on the good wool coat and hat that had belonged to his father, articles of apparel that Shark had coveted. The coat fit too loosely, he noticed. But the small cracked looking glass revealed that the hat became him.

He selected a tub of salt herring that seemed especially choice and told his mother he would dispose of it for her. Then he asked Kip to lend a hand in carrying the fish to Navy Yard.

"But clean yourself up," he requested. "We haven't seen Susan Stokes for a good while."

Kip was agreeable. He washed sketchily and donned his only unpatched shirt. On his head he placed at a rakish angle the cap his mother had recently knit for him.

Wapping seemed friendly as the boys made their way through its crowded lanes. East Smithfield smelled pleasantly of beef being pickled at Navy's victualing works. Tower Hill aroused no shudders, for they rarely thought of the ghastly things that had happened there. (Executions of queens, and of nobles grown too powerful, all pious or gallant at the last, with never a quaver of fear.) For that was long ago, remote from the bright sunshine of today.

At the conduit they stopped and drank some water, changed hands and went on. Each was happy in his own way. They were forgetful of their father's death. After all, he had been more at sea than at home; they were accustomed to his long absences. Ended now was the steady ache of sorrow that had afflicted them for a while like a dreary blight. Whatever grief awaited them henceforward would come in flashes; as when they might see a father and his lads in comradeship, or might hear laughter that sounded like Tom Skeet's, or would notice a sailor entering his house with a sea bag on his shoulder.

"Watch out, Kip!" Amos exclaimed. "Hide the tub!" They were in Hart Street, nearing Seething Lane. With dexterity they stowed the little tub in the matted boxwood hedge of St. Olave's burial yard and stood nonchalantly in front of it. A bailiff was approaching. Kip yawned. Amos scratched his elbows.

The bailiff eyed them, saw two clean but aimless boys watching a flight of starlings. "Hey, there, ye bigger one!" he called. "Ye must be 'prenticed. Does master know ye're loiterin'?"

"I'm on an errand," Amos replied, then added disrespectfully, "any objections, old nosy?"

It was the way an apprentice might speak, that being their way of proclaiming they were not slaves but freeborn young males bound out to learn a craft; if seven years seemed "horrid long," at least it was not forever. Now and then apprentices went abroad at night in swaggering bands and tore down shop signs, though as a rule they limited their defiance to saucy repartee. Amos sometimes envied them the bravado they found in being attached, even so humbly, to the City guilds, in being organized as "we" and "us," though he would not have traded his independence to attain it.

The bailiff passed by, and when he was out of sight the Skeets picked up the herring tub and went their way.

Mr. Pepys' house was one in a row of tall dwellings in Navy Yard, most of them occupied by officers, all within sight of Navy Office. The houses had but small kitchen yards, and none had a drying green or a stable, for the area around the Tower of London was congested.

In the Pepys back yard they saw a tall girl with pale gold hair, fastening a leash on a spaniel dog. Amos walked more erectly at sight of her, but it was Kip who made a remark.

"It's that girl again," he muttered. He meant the Lady Anne Montagu. Last October they had encountered her here, drying her long hair. She had hardly noticed Kip but had looked at Amos admiringly, talking to him about the weather and the boats on the Thames. She said it was exciting to visit at Cousin Sam Pepys' house because it was so close to the Tower and the Bridge. She told of a boating jaunt she had gone on with Cousin Elizabeth Pepys. Amos had been so taken with her, staring at her silky hair and listening to her voice, that he almost failed to speak to Susan Stokes when she came to hang out the dish towels.

Amos was gratified to see Anne Montagu again—he had learned her name—and, this time, was better prepared. He doffed his father's hat smartly; his own yellow hair was nothing to sneeze at. Lady Anne studied him as if for a portrait.

"It's you," she said. "You've brought the salt herring. Cousin Elizabeth's been expecting it. I asked for salt herring for breakfast, and she said there wasn't any. She said, 'Maybe the boys from Dick's Shore will bring it this morning, then you can make a snack of it.'"

"Do you like the stuff so much?" Kip asked in surprise.

Seeming not to hear, she continued to glance at Amos. She adjusted a comb with a supple white hand. With the other hand she expertly held the dog's leash.

"Things happened to keep me at home," Amos said. "I'm late with all my deliveries." He looked at his tub of fish and wished they were vegetables or flowers. "Is Susan Stokes about?"

"I think so. You've brought your brother, I see." She was making talk as if they were social equals.

"Yes, he helps me carry the load. His name's Kip Skeet."

"What an odd name!" she exclaimed, continuing to look at Amos.

"It's Dutch," Amos said stiffly. "He was named for our Dutch grandfather."

"Well, it might be worse. I had an old relative named—if you'll believe me—Apollo Pepys. That sounds rather silly, even on a tombstone. You'd much better be named Kip Skeet, I should say."

Kip touched his cap, glad to be noticed in any way at all. "Thank you, ma'am! Can I take that dog off your hands?"

She turned to him with a bright smile. "Oh, would you, for a few minutes? I promised Cousin Elizabeth I'd lead him around Navy Yard. He gets languid if he's not led about. "Here!" She gave Kip the leash, and he set off proudly.

That left her alone with Amos. "I wonder if you want to

see Susan Stokes right away? She's trussing up some fowls."

"I can wait," Amos answered, then added, "Lady Anne."

"Must you be in the fish trade all your life?" she asked him.

"No. I'll soon have better work. Something higher." (Amos heard himself with surprise.) "I've got prospects, you understand."

"Oh?"

Amos felt that he must tell something of grandeur about himself. But what? His father's death, of course. There would be no deception there, nothing false or exaggerated. "Did you hear about the *London* going down at Lea Roads?" he asked her.

"Oh, I did! And last month when we went down to the Hope on a barge, Cousin Elizabeth and Paulina and I, we saw the place where it happened. I imagined the water was darker there, and a sad wind was blowing. We girls were nervous all the way to the Hope and back, but we were especially frightened when we neared Lea Roads. We could picture the *London* lying down there, just under the water."

"Our father, Thomas Skeet, was a seaman on the *London*."

"Was he one of those saved?" Anne asked quickly.

"No, he wasn't."

She gave an anguished little cry and came toward him. He saw that her eyes had filled with tears. "Poor Amos and Kip," she murmured, and her lovely voice was sincere. She put her hands on his shoulders and gently kissed his mouth, and laid her cheek for a moment against his cheek, and he thought he would never again feel the like of that pitying caress.

The scullery door opened, and Susan Stokes stood there in a soiled apron, looking at them in blank surprise. Her eyes seemed as big as saucers. The Lady Anne turned away from Amos, but not in haste. As usual, she moved with measured grace, as if life itself were a minuet, and she must step it off. "Susan," she reported sadly, "Amos's father went down on the *London*."

"Mercy on us," Susan said in a stricken voice, but nothing else came from her, not so much as a gesture. For even greater than the shock of this news was the shock of seeing Anne Montagu fondling Amos Skeet in the kitchen midden. Things were worse than she had thought.

"What did you do with Mrs. Pepys' little dog, Lady Anne?" she asked in a toneless voice.

"Amos's brother took it to walk," Anne replied. "I see them coming back now." She went to meet Kip on Admiral Batten's premises, an area with fewer cinders and more shrubbery than the Pepys yard, and took the leash from him. "Thank you, Kip," they heard her say in her lilting voice. "Will you have this gold ring from me?"

"I don't want any pay," Kip protested, but he looked at the ring with a good deal of interest.

"It's not to pay you for anything, Kip. Sometimes rings are given when there's been a death. You've lost your father, so here's a ring in memory of him."

"It ought to be the other way," said Kip, who was no fool. "It's the family of the person buried that gives out rings."

"Take it, please!" Lady Anne commanded, and Susan and Amos saw her drop it into his hand. You would never have guessed she was but fourteen years old. She took the dog's leash and went toward the front of the premises, looking back at Amos with a gentle smile as she passed under a brick arch.

"Amos," Susan exclaimed, "I'm sorry about your father!" She longed to say comforting words to him, suitable words. She wanted to embrace him and say, "See, Amos, I'm weeping for you!" But she could not express herself by word or tears, for Anne Montagu's performance had shut her off, and now she was a spring gone dry.

"Is the herring the same price as usual?" she asked.

"The same," Amos answered.

"Will you bring it to the scullery, the way you usually do?"

"Yes, Susan, I will." Like a person in a dream, Amos picked

up the little wooden tub and took it indoors and emptied the contents into a firkin which Mr. Pepys kept for his pickled herring. Susan took some coins from a shelf in the kitchen and gave them to him, and he dropped them into his pocket.

"Won't you count them?" Susan asked tartly. "Maybe I've held out twopence for myself."

He shook his head in negation to the idea that she would cheat him, unaware of her sarcasm.

"Well—" she said uncertainly.

"Susan, I've got a good deal to tell you, but not now."

"Next Sunday, then, Amos? That's five days off. I could go for a walk with you at one o'clock. I could bring some food in a basket. I'll have a half day off because Mr. and Mrs. Pepys will dine at the Penns'."

"Do you mean you want to go on an outing, Susan?"

"Yes, that's what I mean. Where should we go?"

"Any place away from the river," Amos answered. "I get tired of sight and smell of old Thames."

"Lincoln's Inn Fields, then?"

"That's a far piece, and it's full of swells."

"No place is too good for us, Amos. Lots of places are too bad, but none's too good." She added reluctantly, "Bring Kip if you want to. There'll be enough lunch."

Amos brightened. "Thank you, Sue. I hate to leave him on the docks by himself very long. Where must we meet?"

Susan considered, named Aldgate as convenient to all. "We can walk through Cornhill and Cheapside, cut through Paul's Church Yard to Ludgate, and come out in Fleet Street. We'll stop and see my mother, if you're willing? She lives just off Fleet Street."

"It sounds all right to me," Amos said, "but it's a long trip. We'll need to come home by water." He scratched his elbows and calculated. "I can pay for that."

Susan almost offered to pay her share of the barge fare home, then caught herself. She would be providing food for three.

Let Amos assume a gentleman's part, or they would all be shamed.

Amos whistled at Kip, who was staring at the Pepys house as he always did when they came here. "Let's be going, Kip," he said, and they went away together, both bemused. Kip was thinking of Toby Wayneman, a boy who used to work for Mr. Pepys, and was wondering what had happened to him. He had become their friend after he ran away from Mr. Pepys; then he had got into trouble and had gone out of their lives. Kip wanted now to talk of Wayneman, their lost friend, but he saw it was no use; Amos had other things on his mind.

"I know what's the matter with you," he said to Amos with a shrug. "The wrong girl kissed you."

Amos laughed. "Think so?"

When Susan was putting the dressed fowls on skewers, Anne Montagu came to the kitchen in search of her handkerchief, or so she said. "When is Cousin Sam going to get another cook, I wonder. A woman to replace Besse." Her voice was sympathetic.

"Isn't my cooking satisfactory?" Susan asked with a flounce.

"Oh, yes. But don't you have too much work to do, Susan?"

"Only when we have too much company, Lady Anne."

"If you mean my sisters and me," Lady Anne answered, "we're leaving at once. Our coach is coming to take us away; not just to our father's town house, but all the way to Hinchingbroke. Mother says we've been in London long enough."

"Oh?" Susan felt a rush of gratitude to Lady Montagu. She pictured her fleetingly as a stately woman wearing a halo and a blue silk gown, snipping roses and telling her daughters not to be nonsensical.

"Tell me, Susan," prodded Lady Anne, "is there anything between you and that Amos Skeet? Is there an understanding?"

"No, there's not," Susan answered, dropping the pepper shaker and staring off into space. It was a chilling fact that Amos had never asked her to pledge herself to him—to wait for him, as the saying went, had never spoken to her of his future. Lady Anne stooped and picked up the pepper shaker and handed it to her. "Thank you," Susan said absently.

"Amos is a handsome person," Anne went on, "and he looks cleaner than my brothers. He's not got any blemishes. And what hair there is on his face—well, it's golden."

"Dear me," Susan said, starting to pepper the fowls right viciously. "Why don't you give him one of your father's fine razors? Then he could shave off his golden hairs. They do look rather ready, there on his cheeks."

"He told me he has 'prospects,' Susan. What are they?"

"I've never been so prying as to ask him."

"Well, good-by to you. I'll remember your advice. I'll bring Amos one of the Montagu razors, next time I come here."

"Try to remember we are all pretty young, Lady Anne, especially you."

"Just last month, Susan, Mr. John Evelyn mentioned at our dinner table that his mother was fourteen years old when she married his father."

"And how old was his father?"

"Oh, rather old. Twenty perhaps."

"If you're thinking of eloping with Amos Skeet, Lady Anne, you'll have obstacles. He hasn't got a shilling."

"Don't be absurd, Susan. Why would I consider eloping with a fish boy?"

"Yes, Lady Anne, why would you? But daydreams are strange; they can carry you away. You see yourself in a few years, I expect, eloping with Amos, handsomer than ever, and taking him to Lord Montagu afterward and saying, 'Please make him one of your secretaries, dear Father.' You imagine it would be no trouble at all. Well, I've got news for you, Lady Anne; Amos Skeet can't read."

Anne Montagu blinked in surprise but soon regained her poise. With a smile and a shrug she dismissed the subject. "Good-by for a while, Susan. I like you. Try to like me a little in return, won't you?" She went out of the room in her own peculiarly floating way. Later, Susan saw the three Montagu girls get into their big coach with the crest on it, and a footman tucked them in and put their hatboxes at their feet. She was watching from the brick archway, with an apron around her shoulders, and if Anne Montagu saw her peeping, she was too well-bred to show it.

The day was mild and sunny, April without a shower. Though this rainless year must make history, must soon be shuddered at, today the weather seemed merely benign.

Susan was on time at Aldgate, well turned out in her best dress and carrying the promised basket. She found Amos and Kip waiting for her, and Kip was granted the privilege of carrying the savory-smelling lunch.

The excursion had begun successfully, but their luck was now to be tested. They had not gone far in Leadenhall Street when they noticed they were being followed by two rowdy women who laughed raucously and kept at their heels, yet refrained from passing them. At the approach to one of Leadenhall's markets, deserted now because of the day's being Sunday, the women darted into a stall and began throwing some garbage that was there. It was rotten cabbage, and the three young strollers were pelted lushly before they took to their heels and ran.

The women made profane taunts and repeatedly called, "We'll learn ye!" as they fired their charges. Their language was very low, and to Susan it was hardly understandable, but Amos and Kip got the drift of their remarks without any difficulty: the women were forbidding them to sell fish.

Looking back, Susan and the Skeets saw their tormentors turn down Lime Street toward the river. "Whatever's the matter with them?" Susan panted.

"They're from Billingsgate," Amos told her. "They're fish people—fishwives, they're called. I don't know 'em, but they're after Kip and me for selling salt herring."

"How did they recognize you?" Susan asked. "How would they know who you are, if you don't know them?"

"Somebody must've put 'em on to us," Amos said, puzzled. "Come to think of it, a pair of rough women were at Dick's Shore yesterday, and when they went to Nokes' wharf, Mr. Nokes got rid of 'em. They kept looking at our boat. I don't know why."

Amos glanced back uneasily, and as he did so he saw an agile male figure enter a market stall and disappear. The man reminded him of Shark, in his quick movements. But then, he had several times imagined such a thing without confirmation of any sort. He had hoped devoutly that Shark had not been drowned at his hands, but now the menace of the man, vengeful and mischievous, changed the trend of his emotions. "Let's hurry, Susan," he said. "Come on, Kip, let's not hang around here. We can clean ourselves up when we get to Cheapside."

But Kip had to retaliate. Darting back, he picked up a rock the size of a turnip and hurled it at the women. He hit one of them expertly and brought on another outburst of profanity. "Hey, fishwives," he yelled, "go wash out your mouths!"

Amos cuffed him and ordered him to desist. "I tell you, Kip, and I mean it, let those creatures alone!"

Cheapside was pleasantly lively, for law-abiding folk dwelt above their shops, and the street was so wide and interestingly furnished that it resembled a carnival. Jewish and Christian merchants mingled here to advantage, for the Jews had come back from exile during Cromwell's reign and, well traveled and enlightened, were promoting trade and teaching the provincial English to be a nation of shopkeepers.

Cheapside had another convenience for the public, at this moment more attractive than shopwindows. It was a water conduit, a lead-lined reservoir that poured its overflow into a marble trough before sending it on to the Thames. It was fresh, cool water, brought all the way from Hertfordshire. With one accord Susan and the Skeet boys hurried to the conduit. There, at the spill, they began to wash away the garbage, using Amos's clean handkerchief and laughing hysterically.

"You're good-tempered, Susan," Amos said. "Most girls would be making a fuss, I expect. Will you kindly scrub the back of my neck? I can't reach it."

"Bend down and hold still," Susan answered. As she washed Amos's neck at his request, doing a delicate job to spare his shirt, she felt on a par with Lady Anne Montagu, who had kissed him and laid her cheek against his. This too was a caress.

"Now I'll work on Kip," she offered, when she could no longer prolong her services to Amos.

"I've cleaned up my own self," Kip objected.

"Not very well," Susan said. "Your forehead's smeared." She washed his impatient face patiently, for he was Amos's young brother, his pride and his burden. "You look like Amos," she said in surprise, "only softer."

"He'll toughen," declared Amos, "or our name's not Skeet."

Susan suggested that they alter their plans and go directly to the commons, not stopping in Fleet Street until they had had their outing. "I'm too stirred up to talk to my mother now," she admitted. As the prospect of an early meal was highly agreeable to the Skeets, they proceeded to Lincoln's Inn Fields at once.

Amos hurried ahead and chose a spot under an elm tree for their dining place. When Susan and Kip came into sight he piped them to it by whistling his father's favorite chantey. He had driven away a pair of grazing sheep and, with a furze broom he had found, had swept the ground clean of droppings. Overhead, the young elm leaves were like green lace.

Susan was enraptured, for she was one of those fortunate girls to whom simple things give pleasure. "It's the prettiest place in sight," she told Amos. "I wonder how you found it."

It had been something of a feat, for the Fields were alive with folk who had come to enjoy nature in the springtime, or merely to see and be seen. While some rode through in coaches, many walked and carried baskets, intent on finding a place to spread a cloth.

Bordering the great green to the west were the Italian-type villas of the rich, built by the famous architect Inigo Jones. Those houses were separated by brick walls from the open park, aloof and decorative. One would be Lord Montagu's residence. Susan wondered which house it was, though not anxiously, for the Montagu girls were stowed away at their castle near Cambridge, not able to intrude today.

Meanwhile, a limping man in a torn cape and a moth-eaten cap knocked on the door of the sexton of St. Bride's and asked admittance. "Sexton," he said, "I've somethin' to tell ye and yer wife. Be this she? Well, I'll waste no words. Yer daughter, ma'am, Susan Stokes that works in Navy Yard, is in bad company today. She's gone to Lincoln's Inn Fields with two boys of bad repute, name of Skeet."

"Skeet?" echoed the startled woman in bewilderment.

"Yes, ma'am. An unlikely name, I grant ye. These boys 'ave a mother to be pitied—a sailor's widow that lives on a boat at Dick's Shore and conducts a nice little 'errin' trade."

"What else about this woman?" asked the sexton's wife gropingly. "Does my Susan know her?"

The visitor shrugged. "I doubt she does. I only brought up the widow's name to show I know the whole sorry story. It's 'er criminal sons I want to warn ye of."

"Do wait, please!" exclaimed the sexton's wife. "If my child is on an outing with the boys you speak of, I'm sure they aren't ruffians. Susan never liked bad company. She's a good, industrious girl. Her employers will tell you the same thing."

"Then may ye continue to keep 'er good and industrious, ma'am, is my fervent wish fer ye. But she's playin' sister this day to young Kip Skeet, a lad that's as wild as a bat, and to his older brother that's a murderer. Amos Skeet drowned a man at Dick's Shore hardly a month agone. I seen it with my own eyes, though 'twere near dark when he pushed the man in the river."

"Oh, mercy!" moaned the sexton's wife, and she looked at her husband in great distress. She was as faded and weary a little person as you could find, and she was trying to quiet two small children while she listened.

The sexton took over. "If my stepdaughter is mixing with bad company, stranger, we'll put a stop to it. I'll send word to her employers that she'll see no more of those coves. What's your name, by the way?"

"A name ne'er matters, sexton. But it were a good friend o' mine that was drowned by the Widow Skeet's eldest. I'm not seekin' vengeance, mind ye. But I've not been idle, neither. Ye'll be glad to hear as 'ow this dangerous young fellow will be picked up by the press troops, any day now. 'E's ripe fer it. 'E looks to be a seventeen-year-old."

The talebearer smiled, but his smile was a grimace. Susan's mother was repelled and frightened. She was reminded of a ferret that had raided the fowl yard when she was a child.

"What are your plans for the younger boy?" she asked cautiously. "You call him wild. What has he done that's out of the ordinary for a boy to do?"

"Just today, ma'am, I saw this with my own eyes. 'E stoned a couple o' honest fishwives in Leadenhall Street. They was but warnin' 'im not to 'awk fish—a sly 'abit 'e's got. The 'onorable Fishmongers' Company would be interested to know 'e cries pickled 'errin' without a license."

"I hope you won't report the boy." She spoke placatingly, not to anger the stranger. "He's trying to help his widowed mother, I've no doubt."

"I'll not turn 'im in. I'll let things run their course. Little Skeet will be easy 'andled, once 'is brother's out o' the country. A tight bridle fer colt or boy, I always say."

"Something else puzzles me. Surely my Susan's welfare means nothing to you. Leave off being devious, please. Why have you come here? What do you want of the sexton and me?"

The man lowered his bold eyes, cornered for the moment by forthrightness. But he rallied. "Yer fine ami'bility becomes ye, ma'am. Likewise the way ye come to the point. Ye've asked a question. I'll answer. What I want of ye is this. That ye warn yer girl to mind 'er own affairs. She's no doubt soft on Amos Skeet. When the boy's been seized fer Navy duty, don't let 'er bring 'er friends to meddle. And afterward, let 'er forget the younger one. I can manage little Skeet by mysel'." His voice, at first so oily, had become a snarl.

"He's right, wife," the sexton said in a hurry.

"No!" exclaimed the former Mrs. Stokes vehemently. "The man's not right in any way at all." Her spirit, aided by a memory, had risen triumphant over fatigue. "Notice how he's striding about, though when he came in, he was limping. His voice has altered, too. We must not let him browbeat us." She spoke as if he were not there in the flesh, but only in his evil spirit.

"Hold on, wife!" said the startled sexton, for he knew a dangerous man when he saw one.

"I must say what I mean, husband," said Susan's mother, recalling her recollection more vividly. One day, a dozen years ago, she and her father, walking in Fleet Street, had surprised a group of Cromwell's men in the yard of St. Dunstan's. They were examining its windows, beloved by Anglicans. The chief of the intruders, a towering Scot, lifted his sword to break a rare window that offended him, and the old barrister seized the blade and threw it to the ground. "Spare beauty, barbarian!" the frail old man cried out. And the Scot, a misguided man, but reasonable, picked up his sword and sheathed it and led his men away.

This was the memory that had recurred to Susan's mother, and she knew she could not be craven. Young lives are as precious as stained glass, and as easily shattered.

"Be so good as to leave," she said to the stranger who stood glowering at her. "You threaten us, but I'll make no bargain with you, and my daughter won't."

"Are ye deaf to my warnin's?"

"Yes, quite. If that erring lad is deprived of his older brother and is menaced by you, I'll help Susan stand by him!"

With that, she fainted and fell to the floor like a wilted lily, for she was quite anemic.

Shark—for it was he—looked at her prone body with visible relief, shrugged and departed. For a moment, there, she had seemed a person to be dreaded.

Susan's lunch proved adequate—Mrs. Pepys had been generous with a chine of beef and buttered bread—and the meal under the elm was relished. Three jam tarts concluded it. Immediately afterward, Kip said he would take himself off to spend twopence at a puppet show across the common. His only instruction from Amos was to come directly back. This he agreed to do, being already in bad grace.

Susan had the pleasure of being alone with Amos at last. She reminded him of his remark to her in the Pepys kitchen. "You said you had a good deal to tell me, Amos. Is it about your father and how he died?"

"Yes, Susan, that's part of it. But it's mostly about some trouble I got into afterward." He began a meandering recital of what had happened to the Skeets from the moment of the explosion. He spared nothing, not even his mother's tendency toward strong drink, though it shamed him to tell it. He would have liked to have Susan Stokes picture Mrs. Skeet as a paragon of dignity, like the Lord Mayor's wife; or at least like one of those Puritan women who wore plain white caps and rode quietly to Smithfield market beside their husbands.

Susan was dismayed by the news of Mrs. Skeet's erratic conduct. "Do you mean your mother gets beside herself from rum, Amos? Does she forget her own children while she's tipsy?"

"At times she does, Susan." Amos got up and swept the ground around them. "Must you have a fit about it?"

"No," said Susan hastily. "I reckon everybody's parents do

odd things, one way or another." She thought how her own mother had taken for second husband an indolent, ignorant, handsome man who had almost nothing to recommend him. "I've got a very common stepfather," she confided to Amos, "the sexton of St. Bride's. He never strikes my mother, and I think you could call him decent. But he put me out of the house when I was rather young. He'll do scroungy things to turn a shilling. He sells burial room in the church floor after an isle's filled; just has the gravedigger shove aside old bones, to make room. Imagine!"

Amos was encouraged to know that Susan too had an embarrassing relative to endure. "Then you know how it is to wish things were different, Susan."

"Oh yes, Amos! I do, I do! But go on and tell the rest. You found this man called Shark bothering your mother. What then?"

Amos resumed. When he told of knocking Shark overboard, Susan breathed, "Oh, good! Oh, wonderful!" But when he said, "It looks like I drowned him," she exclaimed, "Oh, dreadful! Now you *are* in trouble!"

"In trouble either way," Amos said. "If he's dead, I've done a crime. If he's alive, he'll get even." He finished the story, concluding with his illness, while Susan twisted her handkerchief.

Kip returned to them, and Amos said they must move along. "Do we have to stop at your house, Susan?" he asked her, for he was in no mood to go there.

"Please, let's do, Amos. I've not seen my mother in a long time. It's hardly out of our way at all. Then we can go down to Blackfriars Stairs and take the barge." Seeing that Amos agreed, if grudgingly, Susan was content. She longed to see her mother; she wanted her mother to meet Amos.

When they reached St. Bride's Church in Fleet Street, Susan led them through a wicket and along some pavements. The close of this ancient little church was used for burying the dead and for housing the living. Susan obligingly pointed out the grave of notorious Mary Frith, whose funeral she vaguely remembered. "She was called Moll Cutpurse," she explained. "And over there"—designating a narrow brick house—"is where Mr. John Milton, the great poet, used to lodge."

"Never mind about him," Kip said. "Tell about Moll." He had been dragging his feet, but now he perked up.

"She was every kind of a robber, you know. When she was young she was called 'Roving Girl' or 'Roaring Girl'—I don't know which. Moll was mad about royalty. They say she never robbed any friends of the exiled Stuart, but she'd empty the pockets of Commonwealth men, every chance she got. Once she waylaid General Fairfax on Hounslow Heath and was sent to Newgate Prison for it. But she paid her way out. After that, she settled down in Fleet Street, right next to the Globe Tavern. She was what you call a fence. She received jewels and watches from highwaymen; then she'd sell them back to the rightful owners."

"Why was she allowed to do that?" Amos asked.

"I'm sure I don't know," Susan said. They discussed for a few moments the strange world of adult legality that might punish a boy with ten lashes for taking a loaf of bread, but could overlook Moll Cutpurse's strange traffic and even call it a convenience.

In the shadow of the church's vestibule was a small stone cottage with a slate roof and a pair of crazy dormers with patched panes. It had a damp look, even in a dry season, and was like something left over from Queen Bess's time. It seemed to be the least desirable house in the yard, but there Susan took them.

"I've shown you where we used to live in Chancery Lane," she said to Amos, "my grandfather's good lodgings. Now I must show you what we've come down to. There's only three rooms and a garret to this house, and you can smell Fleet Ditch here, whether the tide's in or out."

Amos saw that the house was smaller than the Skeet houseboat, and more confined. The appraisal made him more appreciative of his floating home on the Thames.

It seemed that the sexton was expecting them, a situation which surprised Susan. "So these are the boys you've been to the Fields with!" he exclaimed. "Let me have a good look."

Susan presented Amos and Kip as politely as possible, but the sexton of St. Bride's continued to block the doorway. "Now see here—" he began, scowling at Amos; but he got no further, for his wife called out, "If it's Susan and the boys, please let them come in, husband!"

They all entered, and Susan and her mother embraced. "We've not long to stay, Mother," Susan said. "I must hurry back to Navy Yard and cook supper."

"Yes, hurry you must, Susan. You must get there before dark. So these are your friends? Some boys you've been on an outing with?"

"Yes, Mother. They're very good friends of mine, Amos Skeet and his brother Kip. I've known them half a year, but it seems a good deal longer." She laid her cheek against Amos's sleeve, blushed in surprise at herself, stood erect.

Susan's mother studied the boys with intensity, while they considered her with curiosity. They were astonished that she was so pale and wan, and that her voice had the sound of a lady of quality. Amos thought her way of speaking was like Anne Montagu's, though with less life.

Their estimating of each other was interrupted by the sexton. He took his wife by the elbow. "Do your duty," he said scoldingly. "Tell these rogues what you've heard about 'em. Lay it on proper, or I will."

"Yes, I must, husband. I like their faces very much, but I must bring the accusations." Then she said unhappily to Amos, "There was a stranger here today who said you'd pushed a friend of his into the Thames and drowned him. Could it be true?"

It seemed that Amos was never going to answer, so Susan spoke. "Amos was protecting his mother when he did it. He wanted only to get the man off his boat—a person called Shark, who wasn't to be trusted. He didn't aim to drown him. Speak up, Amos, and tell my mother how it was!"

"I thought Shark could swim," Amos stated miserably, and that was all he had to say.

It sounded like a poor defense, yet it somehow satisfied the anxious woman who listened. She thought it was commendable that he was contrite and tongue-tied rather than heedless and glib. If he was distressed over taking a life, even a wretched life, then he was a boy of conscience, already a responsible person. "Let us sit down while we talk," she said, for she was not able to stand, and there were chairs and stools to go around. She noticed how Amos placed himself near Susan; and the way he looked at Susan from time to time told that he admired her. As for Susan's feelings toward him, they were in her face and in her voice: she doted on him.

The frail woman sighed, accepting the end of a dream. She had clung to the hope of sending Susan to her cousins in Essex, the only relatives she had, and asking them to find her a husband of good birth. She could picture Susan as the wife of a comfortable squire, or of a young barrister, or of a rector with a country parish. Now, all at once, those hopes seemed remote and artificial. Susan must find her destiny on a lower level. With this lad, perhaps; this decent waterside boy whom she so obviously adored. He was not forward or quick, but he seemed strong and kind. Susan might do worse.

"Is there anything more to tell us, Mother?" Susan asked.

"Yes, there is, Susan. The stranger that came with this tale said Amos will soon be picked up by the press troops. Of course that's legal now. Any one living near Bridewell knows it is." She referred to a great grim building on the Thames, a few blocks to the south of them, over against the Wall. It was a workhouse, and a jail for transients. Here the impressed men were detained a few hours before being put into barges and taken down to the Fleet. Here their women came, storming and pleading for their release.

"And after you've been impressed, Amos," continued Susan's mother, "this man expects to take charge of your brother Kip."

"Mrs. Stokes—if I can call you that—what did he look like?"

"He was a repellent sort of person, Amos. He feigned to be older than he is. He pretended to limp, but presently he forgot and became agile. His cape was ragged, yet I saw a flashy vest underneath it. His smile was horrid, for it wasn't real."

"Did you notice his teeth?" Amos asked.

"Yes. His teeth were very white and pointed."

At these words Kip began to whoop and to pommel Amos with his fists. He turned a somersault and tossed his cap, and then went into a jig he had learned from an Irish sailor.

"Excuse Kip, Mrs. Stokes," Amos said. "It's because of how you pictured that man. It was the Shark himself."

Kip continued to jig in a frenzy of glee, freed of a great dread. Amos's crime had weighed heavily upon him, the more so because he dared not talk of it. Last night he had wakened in the small hours, sweating and groaning, having dreamed that his beloved brother was to hang on Tyburn Hill for Shark's murder.

"Whee!" Kip yelled, prancing and cavorting.

The sexton laid hold of him and shook him. "Quiet down, you rock-throwing pest! You've got sins of your own. Your family's got no call to celebrate. It would be better for all concerned if that man had drowned like he pretended."

"No," Susan's mother said, "it wouldn't have been. Amos has a clean page now." Then she questioned the quiet boy: "Has your father been long dead? Was he always a sailor?"

"I can't remember when he wasn't a sailor," Amos told her. "He died a couple of months ago. He was on the *London*."

"Oh. That's sorrow for all of you. Perhaps you plan to enlist when you're older, Amos? To take up where your father left off? Enlisted sailors are better treated than impressed men."

"No, ma'am. I don't feel any call to fight Holland. It's just a war about shipping. Some of our sailors are going over to the Dutch because the Dutch Navy feeds you better and pays regular. I'd not do that, never. But I won't be seized and throwed in a ship's hold, either."

"*Thrown* in a ship's hold," corrected Susan gently. "Let's be going, Amos. But not by barge, the way we planned. Let's take a hackney coach at Ludgate. It'll cost more than we figured, but I'll pay my share as far as Navy Yard."

"All right," Amos agreed. "Then Kip and me will leg it home from there."

Susan kissed her mother and put a coin into her hand. It was a crown, worth five shillings. "I want you to have it, Mother," she whispered. "Lady Jemimah Montagu, a visitor, left it for me because I ironed her dresses. Mrs. Pepys gave it to me yesterday."

"Thank you, daughter. It's a godsend. The little ones need beef broth."

"And so do you!" said Susan fiercely. "So do you!" She went away with tears stinging her eyes because her mother was growing to be such a shadow.

But in the hackney coach she was gay again, and so were Amos and Kip. They felt riotously extravagant and quite elegant as they clattered eastward through the City, for none of them had ever hailed a hackney coach before. They were wary but unafraid, three against London.

Kip kept calling to the coachman in an affected voice, "Faster, my good fellow!" and pretended to take snuff, while Susan and Amos laughed at him. Now and then, Amos would pretend to see Shark and would wave him a greeting out of the window. "Come and get me, Shark!" he would call out. "I've heard you're looking for me, Shark! Is my bunk ready at Bridewell, Shark?"

Susan, with no properties to help her act except a folded piece of paper, threw herself languidly against the cushions and fanned herself, pretending to be a woman of fashion.

She knew all about such, for it was her fate to hear Mr. and Mrs. Pepys continually gossiping.

"I'm Lady Castlemaine," she drawled. "I've got the finest petticoats in England!" She raised her skirt to show her own clean slip, which actually had a skimpy little ruffle on it, and she kicked up her heels daintily.

"Who's Lady Castlemaine?" Kip asked, taking snuff again.

"She's the beauty King Charles likes too well. Now and then he gives her all the revenue from a ship. He's given her a title too." Then Susan sat erect and tall. "Now I'm Mrs. Stewart."

"Who's Mrs. Stewart?" Amos this time. He was entertained.

"She's a Scotch lovely, very regal looking. The King's going to put her face on a coin as Britannia. She's got a beautiful little Roman nose, Mr. Pepys says." Susan altered her own nose by pinching it. She turned sideways. "See my profile!"

"What's a profile?" Kip asked.

"A half view, stupid."

Amos became serious and self-conscious. "Maybe you can tell me, Susan; are all the nobility greedy and light?"

"From what I pick up at Navy Yard," Susan answered, "those who live at Court are. The royalty too, all but poor Queen Catherine. The things I hear Mr. and Mrs. Pepys tell! It would shock my mother. She doesn't have an idea what an earful I get."

"I was wondering about the Montagus," Amos said.

"Oh? . . . Well, Lord Montagu is right racy. Mr. Pepys says there's a woman named Mrs. Beck—" Then Susan forced herself to add honestly, "But Lady Montagu and the children are as nice as can be. They live in the country and have garden parties and county balls, with the clergy there. The girls sew for the poor. I expect you're thinking of Lady Anne, Amos?"

"Yes, she crossed my mind."

"You think of her a good deal, I suppose."

"Maybe I do. But it's just curiosity. Who will they marry her off to?"

"How should I know? That kind of people—they marry each other, don't they?"

"I've heard of peers' daughters marrying poor chaps and going to America, to one of the colonies."

"America?" Susan exclaimed, incredulous. "That's a place I've never even thought about."

"Well, I have," Amos said belligerently.

Susan saw that Amos Skeet had been smitten with a fantastic idea about love; he might even try to build on it. She wanted to tell him how absurd it was. She could hardly keep from exclaiming, "Do you think Anne Montagu will look at a wharf boy when her courting days start?" But she dared not risk a quarrel.

They turned off Hart Street into Seething Lane, which was actually quiet, not seething at all, now that night was falling. Navy Office was closed. Commissioners and clerks had departed. Disabled sailors and the widows of sailors had trudged homeward, done with importuning. Across the way, the bell of St. Olave's rang for Evensong. The driver of the hackney coach, instructed, came to a stop, and his three passengers alighted. The girl and the older boy computed the division of the fare. The younger lad broke tender shoots from Sir William Batten's privet hedge and fed the horse. " 'E'll always like ye fer that!" cried the driver, meaning his horse, not Batten, and clattered away.

Susan politely said good-by and knocked on the Pepys door. She was admitted by chambermaid Mary. Mary remarked, "You're late, Suze," looked at her accusingly and departed upstairs.

Susan stood uncertainly in the doorway, wondering if Amos might suddenly think of their hours of comradeship and dash up the steps and kiss her good night. Should she linger a few moments, talking, to see? Or was he indifferent to her except as a girl who often had good food to share, and willing ears to listen with? She turned and looked at him, and it was a thing he seemed to expect, for he was watching her.

"Hey, Susan," he called in a puzzled voice, "are you mad at me for any reason?"

"Should I be, Amos? I'm wondering." The door closed smartly. Amos lingered, scratching his elbows.

"She's mad at you all right," Kip said, "but let's not stand here talking about it."

They began to hurry then toward Aldgate, beyond which lay the outer Tower hamlets and the docks. They wisely agreed to take Ratcliffe Road, well back from the river.

Amos left home the following morning to look for some sort of work that would not take him to the docks or the Victualing Yard. He could no longer show himself at those places because of the press. Though the Fleet had gone out and was now engaging the Dutch, it would soon sail home again, minus seamen who would have to be replaced; for a few would have deserted to Holland; and many of the 'pressed men, unused to the rigors of King Charles' battleships, would have succumbed to exposure and spoiled food. Some, too, would have fallen to the guns; for the new crop of young officers (complained the old Admirals) were ignorant and reckless, and they exposed their ships to enemy fire as if attending a regatta.

The Lime House area had a new industry, a rope yard, and there Amos betook himself to ask for employment. It lay inland a little way and was owned by a man named Margetts.

"I want to work for you, Mr. Margetts," Amos said. "I can start any time. I need work because I'm the head of my family."

"Then you expect pay, boy, while apprenticing?"

"There's no ropemakers' guild, ever I heard of, sir."

"Cording used to be an important London trade," Mr. Margetts countered. "It kept to the rules."

"But not any more, sir, asking your pardon. We both know all the rope yards are outside the City. I've heard they hire any stout hands they can get, and no 'prenticeship's called for."

"So what's your proposition, boy?"

"Say I'll work for nothing a couple of weeks, while I'm catching on. After that, I'd have to have wages, or it's no go." Amos spoke with more boldness than he felt. He stood at his full height, hoping he looked rugged and able.

Margetts hardly hesitated, for here was an intelligent young male, strongly built and not afflicted with a cough. Margetts was expanding his rope walk, having been promised a large order of rope for the Fleet. Mr. Pepys of Navy Yard had bespoke it, saying the King's Yards at Chatham and Woolwich were hard put to supply rope for the ships in wartime.

"I'll try you on," he told Amos, "and pay you two shillings a day after the second week. Be here at seven tomorrow morning in any old clothes you've got. Grease your nostrils well, and bring a handkerchief, if you've got one." When Amos looked puzzled, he said shortly, "Hemp's dusty."

Amos went home, elated. It seemed that his worst problems were about to be solved: he would soon be earning money to feed the family, and he would not have to show himself at the docks. But after explaining this to his mother and Kip, he remarked that two shillings a day hardly made a fortune; the salt-herring trade could not be given over.

"We'll have to make our deliveries at night," he told Kip, "after I get home from the rope yard."

Mrs. Skeet protested. "Ye'll be too tired, son! Kip and me can make the deliveries. I'm not too weak to take hold of a little tub, nor too proud, neither. Especially when a child o' mine has got the other handle."

"Well, we'll work it out, one way or the other," Amos told them. "But let's settle one thing here and now. We'll not carry any more fish inside the City, not even around Tower Hill. No use to anger the Fishmongers' Company."

"Not even to the Pepys house?" Kip asked in disgust.

"You heard me, Kip."

"I hate to lose that order," Mrs. Skeet complained, running her hand through her hair and worsening its untidy condition.

"Mother," Amos requested, "will you please comb your hair and pin it up neat? You look like a scarecrow."

"So ye're ashamed of your old muvver, are ye? Can a woman pickle herrin' all day and still look a fine lady? Oh, the ingratitude of children!"

"And pull up your stockings," Kip begged when their mother paused to catch her breath. "Put on your garters, to hold 'em up."

Sobbing dramatically, Mrs. Skeet left the deck and went to the little cabin that was her bedroom. The boys could hear her exclaiming, "Oh, the cruelty of men-children! Oh, why didn't heaven send me daughters with kind tongues instead of the monsters I've got? Oh, the pity of it!"

"She's not been this stirred up in a long time," Kip muttered. "What's she about to do?"

"She's about to wash her face, I hope," Amos answered. Sure enough, there came the welcome sound of Mrs. Skeet pouring water into a basin from a pewter pitcher that she had, and then a good deal of splashing.

Amos sighed. "I hate to hurt her feelings, but it ain't kind to let her go careless and dirty. Our dad wouldn't want it. It's a habit she got into when she—"

"Go on and say it, Amos. When she tippled."

"Yes, when she drank spirits. But she hasn't taken a drink since the *London* went down. She's trying hard, Kip. Admit it."

Kip nodded, dismissed the subject. He had another worry—the trial of doing without Amos's company in the days ahead. "You know what, Amos? I think I'll look for work, myself."

Amos started to protest, held his tongue. There was plenty of work for Kip to do at home—helping at the brine tubs, scrubbing the quarters, delivering the herring—but it was all mighty tedious. If the boy could pick up some odd jobs on the outside that would interest him, better to let him and wish him well. Besides, every extra sixpence would help.

"Have you got anything in mind?" Amos asked him.

"There's a farmer down at Isle of Dogs that let me drive his horse and cart last summer while he spread manure. He didn't pay me, but I was younger then."

"I remember. A man named Stubble. Well, the first day you're not needed here at home, Kip, go down there and apply, if you want to. But don't expect big pay."

"I'm not needed tomorrow," Kip decided.

Amos had hardly left the house the following morning when Kip prepared to do the same. Mrs. Skeet had been made acquainted with her younger son's intention of finding some work, but she had not expected such a hasty pursuit of the plan. While she was still demurring, Kip kissed her good-by —a rare salute on his part—told her his destination, and took off.

He cut inland and eastward and after an hour's walk arrived at an area of small farms. The Isle of Dogs was not an island but a peninsula, downstream from Lime House. The Thames River encircled it on three sides. Directly across the river was Greenwich—the castle, the park, the town—where the Tudor rulers used to reside at certain seasons. If you should follow the Thames River around the Isle of Dogs you would trudge all morning and come to the docks of Blackwall, where the Navy laid its masts; but if you crossed the peninsula by land, there would be nothing to it. Parts of the Isle of Dogs were marshy, parts arable; and on its upper reaches abounded poplar trees of great size.

Kip found Mr. Stubble in his hayfield, looking doleful. It merely annoyed him that Kip asked for work.

"Git on with ye, boy," he said, "I've got no need for any 'elpers. There's been no rain for months, as ye might 'ave noticed. Winter was the worst in my memory for ice and frost, but ne'er a good snow. Ground's 'ard an' dry. Won't make enou' hay to pitch. Won't nurture the corn we dropped. Won't sprout vegetables."

"Why don't you spread manure, Mr. Stubble," Kip suggested hopefully, "like last year?"

"Without water, lad, nothin' serves. Both my cisterns 'ave gone dry. Dig a well, I'd catch salty water. All the farms are bone dry, clear to Walthamstow." Mr. Stubble paused to pick up a clod and throw it at a thin little hound that was regarding them with sad eyes while wagging a cheerful tail. "Git on with ye!" he shouted. "'Ow many times must I clod ye?"

The dog retreated a piece but continued to look and wag.

"Is that a rabbit hound?" Kip asked.

"Yes, 'tis, but his breed's unusual game. They'll fight a badger an' bark at a boar. They've been 'ere since the Queen's time, I've 'eard tell. Queen Bess's singin' beagles, they used to be called. Isle o' Dogs got its name because the Tudors kept their 'unt packs kenneled on this side. The buckhounds and the greyhounds 'ave all gone, but some o' these 'ere singin' beagles are still around."

"Why don't you want 'im?" Kip asked.

"Got three old 'ounds now. Can't take care of 'nother one. Wife won't 'ave it."

"Don't anybody want 'im?" Kip eyed Mr. Stubble probingly.

"It looks like you do, boy. Whistle 'im after ye. 'E's not got his growth. If 'e gets too hungry an' eats fowls, 'e'll be clubbed. Ye'll be doin' a kindness to whistle 'im away."

Kip approached the dog. It retreated and crouched servilely but kept hopeful eyes fixed on him. Kip turned toward home and whistled softly. The little hound got up and followed, its short legs bounding, its long ears flopping. Kip walked on, not looking back. When he came to a group of poplar trees near the roadside he paused and took his lunch from the pocket of his smock. It was salt herring between two slabs of bread, intended for his noontime repast. "Here, Singer!" he invited. "Come and eat fish! Might as well get used to it, Singer!"

Singer, newly dubbed, came cautiously, cringed a moment,

devoured the food. Then he stood on his hind legs and attempted to lick Kip's face. "You little old cove!" Kip said happily, tousling him. "I ne'er saw such a good-for-nothin' beast."

Mrs. Skeet was not surprised to see Kip coming home at high noon, but she was puzzled to see him bringing the beagle aboard. A maxim had been pronounced by her and ruefully accepted by the boys that the Skeets could not afford to keep a dog.

"Name's Singer," Kip told her, trying to sound casual. "He's mine. Mr. Stubble hasn't got any work for me, but he gave me this fine dog. He's just about grown, a rabbit hound, but he's game. Will fight a badger."

"I don't know as I ever saw a badger," said Mrs. Skeet. She always spoke irrelevantly, so Kip was not deceived. She was wondering if it would be possible for the Skeets to keep a dog; she was lowering her sights. While talking of badgers, which she continued to do, saying she'd heard they abounded in Yorkshire, and so on, she was studying the beagle. Finally she held out her hand, palm up, and the little hound went straightaway and licked her fingers. "He's thin," she mourned. "Real skinny. I had a little dog when I was a child, a terrier. Some people in a carriage brought him to the inn. They went away without paying my father what they owed, and they left the dog. It and me took to each other. It was still alive when I married your dad and went away."

"Well, I declare," Kip said.

Mrs. Skeet felt the beagle's ribs to assure herself that he was as thin as he looked, then she said with unaccustomed composure, "After ye've fed this little hound o' yours, Kip, make 'im a bed on deck. Make it aft, so he can come and go. He's used to his freedom, I reckon."

Kip again saluted his mother, kissing her forehead with a resounding smack. "You look real neat, Muvver," he said with honest approval. "You look comely."

"Hush, ye!" Mrs. Skeet exclaimed. "That's beguilement,

so I'll tolerate your dog!" However she knew her appearance was at its best today. She had forgiven her sons their criticisms, had wistfully tried to improve her looks.

Susan was almost out of her mind for news of Amos. As two weeks passed, and then a third, she thought that she must have offended him mortally. She had shut the door in his face, she remembered. She had not slammed it, no; but she had closed it in a fit of pique and cut him off before he was through talking. Or was he? Anyway, she should have listened, to find out. Perhaps he was about to say, "This has been the happiest day of my life, Susan, from start to finish!" And yet, he would hardly have declared himself so fancily, especially as there had been that garbage episode. Maybe he was only about to say, "Can you go on an outing again next Sunday, Susan?" That would have been worth hearing. It would have sounded more musical, in spite of Amos's changing voice, than one of Mr. Pepys' song sessions.

Only last night Susan had lain awake listening to a quartet singing up on the leads (as Mr. Pepys called his flat roof). There was Mercer, who was Mrs. Pepys' companion; and Tom Edwards, who was the Pepys page; and Mrs. Knipp, a friend of Mercer's who sang at the theatre; and Mr. Pepys himself. Their voices had sounded heavenly. Now and then Mrs. Pepys would join in, because it frightened her to be left out of things, but her voice hardly mattered; it was true, but it had no strength. As Susan fell asleep, listening, she dreamed that they all came to her and offered to sing at her wedding to Amos Skeet. If the wedding was to occur, her dream failed to tell; but at least the singers had been cordial to the idea, and willing.

One morning Mrs. Pepys remarked to Susan in the kitchen, "We're out of herring. What's become of those fish boys?"

"Oh, I don't know, ma'am!" Susan replied with such passion that Mrs. Pepys was startled. "It could be they'll never come again!"

"Then we'll send to Billingsgate for our cured fish," Mrs. Pepys decided. She noticed Susan's stricken look and exclaimed, "Susan, has that older boy, Amos, caught your fancy?"

Susan nodded mutely.

"You can do better than that, I'd think!" Mrs. Pepys scolded. She was half French, named Elizabeth St. Michel until she had changed her name at fifteen to Elizabeth Pepys. "No matter how ordinary your stepfather is, Susan, you were well born. Try to remember that. Your mother's a gentlewoman, and Stokes is a good name. Can't you aim higher than a fish family when you wed?"

Susan might reasonably have answered, "How can I meet anybody higher in your kitchen, Mrs. Pepys?" But that worldly idea did not occur to her. Her only response was the unuttered query, Where could I find anyone as dear to me as Amos?

Mrs. Pepys, receiving no audible answer, enlarged on her worldly advice. "I married for love, myself," she confessed. "We were poor and had to live in a garret for a while. But Sam was a young man of talents, and he had Lord Montagu, an important relative. I doubt if your fish boy has got either talents or connections. It may be he doesn't even have *l'ambition*."

Susan had to smile. "Oh, he has ambition, I think. He'd like to marry a peer's daughter and go to the colonies."

Elizabeth Pepys laughed. "That's delicious, Susan! I'm glad you can make a joke. That sort of thing shows real wit."

"It wasn't intended that way, Mrs. Pepys."

It was Kip Skeet who finally came. One morning he appeared in the kitchen yard when Susan was sitting on the scullery doorstep, polishing a silver dish. Susan's heart leaped up, or seemed to. "Where's Amos?" she asked quickly.

"He's working at a rope yard." Kip sat down companionably. "Mr. Margetts' place, not far from us. Gets paid every day."

"Oh! Then you've quit the fish trade?"

"No, we haven't. But Amos won't let us deliver fish in the City any more. Says it's risky, account of Fishmongers' Hall."

"I see. Then Amos won't ever come here again?"

"He'll come sometimes, just to see you. A couple of times he's started, but he's been too tired to clean up and change his clothes. It seems like a rope yard wears you down by day's end and makes you cough."

"Has Amos got a bad cough?" Susan asked, startled.

"He hasn't got a consumption, Susan. But now and again he coughs, right after he gets home. It's the linty off the hemp. Twelve hours a day, Amos walks."

"*Walks?*"

"Yes, Susan. Don't you know cordage houses have rope walks? At first Amos hackled the hemp. I mean he combed it over boards that have studs sticking up. But he was too good for that work, and Margetts put him to walking. Amos and some other men wrap bunches of combed hemp around their waists, then they walk."

"Why?" Susan asked. "To deliver the hemp somewhere?"

Kip laughed. "No, that ain't what they're doing. They fasten some hemp fibers to hooks on spinning wheels. Then they walk backward from the wheels and feed the wheels from the hemp around their waists. That makes the first yarn. A bunch of yarns are twisted together to make what you call the strand. Then the strands are twisted together, and that's called layin' the rope. Sometimes the first fibers are tarred, like for Navy rope. Then it's as hard as all get out."

"No wonder Amos gets tired!" Susan said. She was impressed by his new skill, but she feared for his health. "Have you watched Amos work?" she asked Kip.

"Plenty of times. It's not far from our boat. Once when they were short of hands, I helped unroll the bales. It's the best Riga hemp. That's the kind Mr. Pepys holds out for."

"Mr. Pepys? What's *he* got to do with it?"

"The Navy's short of rope, and Mr. Pepys told Mr. Margetts to make him a batch . . . Hey! my dog's in a fight!"

Kip dashed out of the yard and out of sight. From beyond Admiral Penn's house came the sound of a dog fight and of Kip's voice raised in consternation.

Susan waited. After a while the noise ended, and Kip returned, red and breathless. He was dragging a small hound by the collar. "This here's Singer," he panted, "my dog. He was mixed up with that ratter at the Penns'."

"He was on the other dog's property," Susan reminded him. "I'll get you a piece of twine to lead him with. I don't think you ought to bring him into the City except on a leash, Kip." She went indoors and returned with a piece of small rope. Kip tied it securely to the dog's collar.

"Amos bought 'im this collar," Kip said proudly. "Singer's the first dog we e'er had at the wharf." He then explained the dog's supposed pedigree and told how he had come by him.

Susan was charmed. "Just think! A singing beagle from Queen Bess's pack. I've heard they used to carry them in their saddle panniers till they got to the hunting fields."

"Well, Singer wouldn't need to be carried nowhere."

"*Anywhere,*" corrected Susan absent-mindedly.

Kip nodded, implying that she could have her way. "Singer can run for three or four hours at a time. He goes down to Isle of Dogs real often, where he came from. And he likes to go to Bromley Marsh after muskrats. He'd rather I went with 'im, but if I can't, he'll go by himself. 'Nother thing about Singer, he always comes home before night."

"Wait here," Susan said. "I was about to have a bite to eat." She fetched some bread and butter for Kip and herself, and an ample bone for Singer. "There's a good deal of meat left on that joint," she said. There was, indeed. It had been intended for the soup kettle. If Mr. Pepys had seen where it was going, there might have been "Ned to pay," for he was close-fisted in some ways, and made Mrs. Pepys keep a kitchen ledger.

Susan willingly risked Mr. Pepys' displeasure in order to delay Kip and talk about Amos. "Kip," she confided, "I thought

Amos was staying away because he was mad at me. Thank you for explaining things the way you've done. Did Amos send you here?"

"No, Amos didn't send me. But last night he said, 'I wish Susan Stokes knew why I haven't been to Navy Yard.' Then he rolled over and went to sleep."

Susan tried to be satisfied with that. Amos had spoken her name, had wished her to be informed; it was not much, but it was something. "Kip," she said, "favor me with a promise. When Amos gets home tonight, tell him you've been here. Tell him I'm glad he's found regular work that's not dock work. Tell him"—she hesitated, bit her lip and blurted—"tell him I'll be glad to go to Lincoln's Inn Fields next Sunday and carry a lunch, if he and you will join me there."

Kip showed a flash of enthusiasm, then his face clouded to a look of depression. "That's a stupid thing to plan," he said. "Don't you know about the plague?"

"I've heard the plague's in St. Giles. That's quite a way."

"It's in Chancery Lane now, where we walked. Lincoln's Inn is shut up. You can't go through there any more to get to the Fields." Kip referred to the famous law college, through whose beautiful gate pedestrians were allowed to pass to the park; otherwise you must take the carriage route from High Holborn. "The other law Inns are closing, too."

"How do you know all this, Kip? It's not been printed."

"An old porter at Lincoln's Inn has got a son in Stepney that buys herring from us. The son went to Lincoln's last week to see his father. He said none but servants are left there."

"Where have the students and the masters gone?"

Kip shrugged. "To the country, maybe. Any place to get away from the sickness."

"Then the plague's getting close to St. Bride's," Susan murmured, anxiously aware of the little house in the church yard. "I thought it would stay in St. Giles!"

"I'll be going," Kip remarked. "You'd better think of something else for me to tell Amos."

"Just tell him I said to take care of himself."

"Maybe he'll come here and see you next Sunday," Kip said, as if he might arrange it.

Susan brightened. "Do you think so? I'll have the afternoon off. We've got a new cook coming tomorrow."

Kip was so engrossed with his dog that Susan wondered if he had heard. He tugged at Singer's rope, and Singer reluctantly left his worked-over bone and followed. Good-bys were called. Then Susan buried the bone under an ash heap where it could not attract the attention of Mr. Pepys.

It was Kip's nature to influence his surroundings, and he liked to spread cheer. Remembering Susan Stokes' eager face, he advised Amos to go to see her on Sunday afternoon. "I think she wants to see you a mighty lot, Amos," he said. "Dress yourself and go on. I'll look after Muv'."

"Susan wasn't very friendly the last time we parted company," Amos said. "I'm halfway afeard to risk it."

"That girl thinks the world and all of you," Kip stated. "She's always worryin' about you." Then he added inaccurately, "Susan loves you like her own brother."

"Well, now!" Amos was touched, but not entirely pleased. "I don't know as I want to be her brother."

Having been set in motion by Kip, Amos acted with energy.

Putting aside his desire to loaf that Sunday afternoon, he dressed, went to Navy Yard, and lifted the knocker on the Pepys front door. Happening to answer the knock was Mrs. Pepys' lady in waiting, called by her last name of Mercer.

Amos studied her, very much desiring not to be sent to the back door. Susan had told Amos about Mercer. She lived in nearby Crutched Friars—her father a merchant, her mother and sisters rather high-headed. Mercer was not pretty, but she had a good singing voice and played the viol, and these talents made her valuable to Mr. Pepys.

"What's your errand?" Mercer asked Amos. Though he was very cleanly got up in his best clothes, it was evident to her that he was not socially prominent.

"I've come to see Susan Stokes, ma'am. I'm a friend of hers and want to take her for a walk. I think she's expecting me."

Mercer hesitated, and Amos had an anxious moment. His desire to be accepted at the front door was acute, for this was the Sabbath, and he had not come delivering fish. During the past weeks he had been working excessively hard—indeed, his clothes hung loosely because of his steady toil—and he had mastered a trade. Had he not become a new person thereby?

Mercer smiled, causing her plain features to light attractively. "You're Amos from Lime House! Come inside and wait for Susan. Sit on the settle while I find her."

"Thank you, ma'am, I'll be glad to." Mercer went away to summon Susan, and a great contentment settled on Amos. He had passed a barrier.

Susan came downstairs looking very stylish, Amos thought. She was wearing a large hat that tied under the chin. It was one that Mrs. Pepys had grown tired of and given to her, but it was still fetching in spite of its flowers being crushed. The frock was a striped silk hand-me-down from Mercer.

"Would you like to go to Cheapside?" Amos asked her when they were out of doors. "Or had you rather cross the Bridge to Southwark?"

"The Bridge," Susan chose. "Once Besse and I crossed London Bridge and walked all the way to Redriffe, and back."

Amos laughed. "A shorter trip will do me! I reckon Kip told you about my job. I walk all day, making rope."

"I forgot that! Let's just sit in St. Olave's Yard, then."

"Oh, I have to keep my foot in. Let's cross to Bankside and find a place to eat. Or do you have to hurry back here to cook the Pepys' supper?"

"I won't have to be in a hurry, Amos. Mrs. Pepys has hired a new cook, a grown woman named Alice. She came yesterday, and now I'm just cook's helper again. I'm glad of it. I don't get real wages anyhow, because of my age. Only my clothes and keep. The gift money I get is like alms, and not very regular."

"I'm glad you won't have to work so hard now," Amos said in a protective way.

They crossed the Bridge, taking their time. Where the bridge dwellings permitted, they looked out over London and spotted the places they knew. Nothing untoward happened, except that they saw a sharp-faced little girl trampling a small black and white cat for the fun of it; and Susan slapped the girl and rescued the little cat and carried it away.

"What'll you do with it?" Amos asked her.

Susan had no idea. She said Mrs. Pepys objected to cats because she kept birds. "Maybe I'll find somebody in Southwark who wants it," she said hopefully. Her problem was solved by the little cat itself. At an alley entrance in Southwark it jumped from her arms and joined some other cats of its own size and undistinguished appearance.

"I do believe it lives there!" Susan exclaimed. Her cheeks were as pink as the flowers on her hat, thanks to the cat and the wind on the Thames, and her dark eyes were sparkling. Amos looked at her a second time, thinking her to be improved somehow.

At a shabby but respectable tavern called Beacon Inn they had Stilton cheese, a drink made of lime juice, and new strawberries with cream. "I'm afraid you've spent too much money," Susan said worriedly. "Suffolk cheese would have done!"

Amos was glowing with his first experience of buying a meal for a young lady. Though he found it had cost him half a day's wages, he paid up bravely and remained cheerful.

Outside the inn Susan said, "I think they overcharged you, Amos. I was adding on my fingers under the tablecloth, and it seemed to me the keeper's wife totted twopence too high."

"No, she didn't," Amos said. "I've been getting arithmetic from a Scotchman at the limeworks—Hugh McTarvish is his name. He writes me sums to take home and work out. He even wrote the multiplication table for me, and I learned it while I walked rope."

"Amos, how clever of you! Sometimes Mr. Pepys practices

the multiplication table at home—he has to know it because he buys timbers and deals for the ships—and I must say it sounds frightful. I'd never learn it."

"But you can read and write," Amos said shortly. Conveyed in the words was all the frustration he felt because he himself was illiterate. Then he changed the subject abruptly. "I saw Shark last week!"

"Do you mean you met and spoke to him?"

"Nothing like that. It was about dark. The rope hands had quit an hour before, and I'd been to the limekilns to see Mc-Tarvish. Remembered I'd left my coat at the rope walk, went back for it. Saw a man putting a round of cable in a cart. Watched 'im. It was Shark. Finally I showed myself, and we looked each other in the face before he drove off."

"Oh, Amos. You didn't pursue 'im, I hope?"

"I'm not a fool, Susan. I didn't let on I knew 'im. I went straightaway to the caretaker that lives a piece away. He was eating supper with his wife when I arrived. 'Did you let a buyer carry off a round of cable?' I asked him. He said he hadn't. 'Then something's happened that's not regular,' I told him. We went through the rope house and yard then, and sure enough, a Navy order was missing—some rope for the *Royal Charles*. Nothing else was gone from the whole place, except my workin' gloves. Not my coat. Not any tools, either."

"What do you make of it, Amos?"

"Can't make anything of it but befuddlement."

"You're not surprised that Shark came thieving, are you?"

"Not hardly. But why didn't he take more rope, as long as he had a cart? A person on foot could have drug off one coil o' cable, dry as the weather's been. Any one of us workers could 've done it alone."

"You mean, a worker *wearing gloves*, Amos?"

"Yes, Susan, he'd need gloves to do it." Amos looked at his callused hands. "We make ordinary rope raw-handed. But when it's time to lay cable or drag the coils, nobody does it without thick leather gloves."

"Are your own gloves marked somehow, Amos?"

"All the gloves are. Margetts furnishes 'em, never lets 'em leave the rope house. They're numbered with ink. Mine's seventeen, happens to be the same as my age. Margetts remarked on it when he turned 'em over to me. 'If you're still here next year,' he said, 'and I hope you will be, I'll assign you some new gauntlets marked eighteen.' " Then Amos stopped in his tracks and looked at Susan sheepishly. "I've been slow, haven't I? Shark planned to make the robbery point to me. That's why he took my gloves."

"He wanted to get you in trouble, Amos. Notice how he took the Crown's property. He's trying to ruin you, one way or another. Can Shark be what's called a limb of Satan?"

They discussed Satan then; for like most Londoners, they pictured him as a well-built fallen angel with sly, handsome features and a pitchfork. The Calvinist preachers of Oliver Cromwell had described him so, stating that persons who did his will were extra limbs that enabled him to get about more effectively.

"Amos," Susan said, "supposing Shark to be a limb of Satan, I'd be terrified but for something my grandfather told me when I was a little child. One day I ran to him crying that the Devil was coming, and we must bar the door—some older children had told me so—and Grandfather said, 'Don't be afraid, Susan. The evil one can ne'er come in if you don't make a deal with him.' "

Amos pondered this, admitted, "My mother has a dried hare's foot over the door. She thinks it keeps bad company out."

"And Mr. Pepys carries a rabbit's foot for his health," Susan said. "But there's nothing to it. One day he came home with a bad chill and yelled at Mrs. Pepys, 'This couldn't have happened to me if you hadn't lost my hare's foot!' Mrs. Pepys felt in his pocket, and there it was. He'd been carrying it all the time."

Ambling along Bankside, they passed a bear garden where

bears and dogs were cruelly set at each other, and Susan stopped her ears. They saw pits for cock fights, Clink Prison, and an old playhouse. Had they continued beyond the river's bend they would have come to Lambeth, the house and gardens of the Archbishop of Canterbury, hedged in by sordid tenements. But Amos said they must turn home again, so they altered their course.

At an unlikely place full of vehicles near the Bridge's approach, Amos dragged his feet. Susan demanded, "Why on earth are you stopping here, Amos?"

"I'm not stopping, I'm just looking in," he said. It was the Southwark Posthouse. Hostlers were putting six fresh horses to a big stage in the stable yard, passengers were milling about as if distracted, porters were throwing luggage. "Will Wayneman worked here till he died," Amos said. "He was the brother of Toby, that page of Mr. Pepys' I've told you about."

"A person would think Wayneman was the only friend the Skeets ever had," Susan complained. She felt a loss at not knowing Toby. She had gone to work at the Pepys house several months after he had disappeared. She knew he had been a slender, cocky redhead who could read and write well, deliver messages without making an error, and find his way all over London. His liabilities as a Pepys page were that he was not musical and he picked fights with other pages. Now and then Mrs. Pepys spoke affectionately of him to Susan, and so did Will Hewer, the serious clerk who had a little room on the ground floor. But the other servants were too newly come to have known him. As for Mr. Pepys, Wayneman's name never passed his lips. Perhaps he felt unhappy at having beat the little fellow so often.

The stagecoach with its six horses swept past them, headed for Bristol. It made you want to be on it, going somewhere in a hurry. "Some day I'd like to ride a stage," Amos exclaimed, "clear to York!"

"So would I!" Susan declared, then blushed. She hoped she had not sounded as if she wanted to go *with* Amos to York;

on a wedding journey, for instance. "Or I would just as soon go to Oxford," she amended, hastily choosing another direction. "Where's Kip today?"

"He's taking our mother to Cheapside to see a puppet show. She'd ne'er go by herself. She'd lose her way."

"I'd feel honored to meet your mother, Amos. Another time, bring her with you when we're walking out."

"That's nice of you, Susan. She gets lonesome at the wharf."

Crossing London Bridge, which had famously rough planking, Amos reached for Susan's hand and led her along. They could not think of anything to say to each other, though the penny newssheets reported the English Navy had taken some Dutch prizes, and 'prentices were rioting in Smithfield, and the plague had come now to Westminster.

This is a year you would do well to skip, unless you have a historian's mind and a strong stomach. One cannot say why it happened, unless—as some think—to advance mankind in the science of healing disease, or in the greater science of preventing it. It was the time of the plague.

Susan Stokes and the Skeet family will survive. So will Mr. and Mrs. Pepys and their household, though not untouched; for Samuel Pepys recorded in his diary on September 14, 1665:

(We) *hear that a laborour I sent but the other day to Dagenhams to know how they did there, is dead of the plague; and that one of my own watermen, that carried me daily, fell sick as soon as he had landed me on Friday morning last, when I had been all night upon the water (and I believe he got his infection that day at Brainford), and is now dead of the plague. To hear that Mr. Sidney Montagu [a brother to Anne] is sick of a desperate fever at my Lady Carteret's, at Scott's-hall. To hear that Mr. Lewes hath another daughter sick. And, lastly, that both my servants, W. Hewer and Tom Edwards, have lost their fathers, both in St. Sepulchre's parish, of the*

plague this week, do put me into great apprehensions of melan-
choly. But I put off the thoughts of sadness as much as I can,
and the rather to keep my wife in good heart and family also.

While the hot, dry summer advanced in swirls of dust, London forgot its pride and admitted it was sieged. King Charles and the Court escaped to Salisbury, later to Oxford. Rich folk fled to the various shires; wealthy merchants shut up shop and followed. The higher law courts adjourned. Many ministers forsook their parishes, leaving their flocks to vicars and curates braver than themselves, or to fearless nonconforming ministers, five years suppressed.

War with Holland continued while plague ravaged the Fleet, but all other projects fell away. As trade and manufacture were suspended, citizens had no wages with which to support their families. Untainted food became too dear to be purchased, coal from Newcastle was scarce and high. The City itself lacked money for pesthouses.

London must surely have known anarchy but for four faithful officials who moved among the stricken people to promote sanitation, to organize the physicians and apothecaries, to collect and disburse alms. These available ones were Sir John Lawrence, Lord Mayor, who stayed in his City house; General George Monck, Duke of Albemarle, who lodged in Westminster; William Lord Craven, always to be found in his Drury Lane house, belying his name, spending his private means for the poor and sick; Gilbert Sheldon, Archbishop of Canterbury, who kept to Lambeth's slums as an example to his rectors, both faithful and faithless.

Important naval families moved downriver to Woolwich. In July, Mr. Pepys established Mrs. Pepys and two of their maids —Mercer and Mary—in lodgings there. Remaining in Navy Yard to look after Mr. Pepys and his male helpers were cook Alice and Susan Stokes. When September came in, Navy Office transferred to Greenwich. So, necessarily, did Mr. Pepys. With him went his clerk and his page, both wearing mourning bands.

Susan and Alice were left alone in the house in London to ride out the plague. They were surprisingly composed, considering the peril of the times. Both said their prayers frequently, laughed at whatever they could find to laugh at, ate with a fair appetite such food as they could prepare at home. Susan read some books in Mr. Pepys' study. Alice knitted hose for her sister's children in Islington.

The conditions they faced are best told in a letter written by Mr. Pepys to a family friend, just as he quit the City.

I have stayed in the city till above 7,400 died in one week, and of them above 6000 of the Plague, and little noise heard day or night but tolling of bells; till I could walk Lombard Street and not meet twenty persons from one end to the other, and not above fifty upon the Exchange; till whole families, ten or twelve together, have been swept away; till my very physician, Dr. Burnett, who undertook to secure me against the infection, having survived the month of his own house being shut up, died himself of the Plague; till nights are grown too short to conceal the burials of those that died the day before, people being thereby constrained to borrow daylight for that service; lastly till I could find neither meat nor drink safe, the butcheries being everywhere visited, my brewer's house shut up, and my baker with his whole family dead of the Plague.

Susan was honor bound not to go to St. Bride's to see her mother; Mr. Pepys said she could not come back to Navy Yard if she did. Too many houses in that area wore on their doors the dreaded X in red paint, and the pitiful words in capital letters: LORD HAVE MERCY ON US. None could leave or enter. St. Bride's had an outlying burial ground for its plague victims, and it shared this—a strangely touching hospitality— with neighboring St. Dunstan's parish which had none.

Susan and her mother exchanged messages through an old retired actor named Phipps, who lived in St. Bride's Yard. Mr. Phipps brought Susan the news that two church wardens of St. Bride's had died while attending to their duties; that the rector had fled, but that Mr. Richard Pierson, the curate, remained to comfort and serve the parish. "Sexton and his family," said the old man to Susan's joy, "continue to escape the sickness."

Susan begged Mr. Phipps to tell her anxious mother that she had never felt healthier; that she had good company in Alice; that Mr. Pepys and his page, Tom Edwards, came and went often and kept them in food from Woolwich.

"And if you can remember to tell her one more thing, Mr. Phipps, I'll be glad." Susan looked at the fragile old man, wondering how much his head could carry.

"Try me, girl! If the message gets there, all's good. If it spills on the way, nought's lost but words."

"But important words, Mr. Phipps. They're about somebody I'm very fond of."

"Your sweetheart, girl? Speak out!"

Susan nodded. "If you say 'Amos,' my mother will know who's meant. The last time I went to see her, I told her Amos worked at a rope walk. But he doesn't any more; the place is shut down. Tell her Amos works at Captain Marsh's Lime House, making lime. Tell her he's well, and his family's well. Tell her he comes to see me as often as he can."

The old actor cracked his knuckles, looked profound. "Making quicklime, is he? Aye, there's a calling that's fat!" Then he began to quote from a tragedy in which he had once performed, reciting lines about a repellent graveyard.

"You make Amos's work sound gruesome, Mr. Phipps, but it's not! Quicklime is what protects us now. It makes the burial grounds safe again. It purifies stinking gutters. It's the clean whitewash they put on the walls of rooms where sickness has been."

"Aye, girl, that's pretty! At least you make it sound so. I'll tell your mother all of it, and say you're blooming. Aye, and I'll take her this cheese you've wrapped for her. Is it Stilton?" he asked cunningly.

"No, Mr. Phipps, it's only common cheese. Alice and I made it here at home from Woolwich milk."

"Then I've no taste for it, myself."

Susan was relieved to hear that. She gave Mr. Phipps a rasher of bacon for his breakfast, that being all she could spare.

"Oh, enchanting!" he said. "Now a little sack wine, dear, if you've got any?"

"I don't drink, Mr. Phipps, and Alice takes nothing but small beer."

"Not even in an epidemic? That's careless of you both. Let me quote from Hodges, the great doctor. 'Sack is ranked among the principal antidotes of the plague, whether it be drank by itself, or impregnated with wormwood and angelica.'"

Alice had entered the room in time to hear this skillful wheedling, and she was moved by the eager plea in the quavering voice. "I can't resist 'im," she said to Susan. "I'm going to give the old fellow a bottle of Mr. Pepys' sack, out o' the cellar." This she proceeded to do. "Drink it of an evening with your supper," she instructed. "Drink it slow and sparing."

"It will last me a fortnight," the old man told them, "unless I share it with friends. That decision will be made anon." He went happily away with the gifts, assuring them he would come again. But he never did. He succumbed to the plague a few weeks later, as surely as if he had never had a bottle of fine dry sack to fortify him.

Of little effect, too, was the burning of smudge pots at public gatherings and in sickrooms. It caused coughing, streaming eyes, mental confusion. The combustibles oftenest used were saltpeter, brimstone, amber, and rosin; and many persons denied themselves food in order to obtain them.

But Amos Skeet had a theory, which he expounded to Susan. "Smokes and vapors don't cure the plague, I notice. But maybe they ward it off. Like at our wharf. One day last June, Kip found a little piece of ambergris in the pocket of our dad's oldest coat. We mixed it with brimstone and lime and burned it on a shovel, just to make the air pure. We carried the shovel about, sending the fumes all over. Some rats came scampering out that we ne'er knew we had—little black rats. They left in a hurry. Maybe it's the rats that carry the plague."

"Instead of dogs?" Susan said.

Amos nodded, looking so unhappy that she was sorry she had mentioned dogs. All over London and the outlying parishes, dogs and cats were being destroyed in the belief they carried death. The Skeet family schemed and strove to protect Singer. Kip, roaming with his beagle, had repeatedly saved him from catchers sent out by the constables. Sometimes this was accomplished by physical effort on Kip's part—butting, kicking, fisticuffs. At other times by wile; a foot thrust out to trip the dogcatcher; a "Look at that sailor's parrot!" then the quick rescue when the enemy's head turned in curiosity. But usually fourpence in the catcher's palm sufficed, that being double the pay he received for a dog's capture. There would surely come a time when no pence would be handy, and when Kip's strength would not avail. In view of this, Singer was no longer allowed to run, and he took it with bad grace. Tethered to an iron ring on the deck, he would sing mournfully, celebrating past joys and begging for liberty.

"Singer's a healthy dog," Amos said. "He keeps a cold nose. Every week we give 'im a salt-water bath. His breath's clean."

"If the plague's brought by animals," Susan agreed loyally, "it's more apt to be rats that carry it."

"But how?" Amos asked, drinking the chocolate that Susan had brought him. His hair and eyebrows were dusty with lime, and Susan thought he looked like a beautiful young judge, grown prematurely gray. Nowadays he came to see her directly from the limekilns, without changing his clothes; otherwise he could not have come at all. "It looks like I've got just half the truth."

And so he had. The routing of the rodents had saved his dwelling. He could not know why because certain facts were lacking to him, were unknown even to the College of Physicians.

The little black rats of London persistently reached England by ship from India and China, and they were house-dwellers, fond of human society, as unlike the big brown rats of the gutters as they could very well be. How perfectly the plaster and timber houses of old England suited them! They learned to live like mice, with even less stir and damage to property. But they were hosts to the plague-carrying fleas of the East, passing the fleas to human beings in fetid tenements.

Such tenements abounded outside the City on undrained and uncoveted land. St. Giles-in-the-Fields was a place where London had dumped its garbage for centuries. Its laystalls were notorious. Yet folk dwelt in St. Giles; its filthy lanes and rookeries were crowded with the dispossessed, and here the bubonic disease spread swiftly. Cripplegate, without and within the Wall, was another heavily visited area, for into it drained the laystalls of Moorfields. Along dirty Holborn Road and sluggish Fleet River, the dread sickness moved relentlessly; and thus it reached St. Bride's parish and Blackfriars. Southwark was afflicted along much of its waterfront. Finally, when the pestilence had come raging to Ludgate and Bishopgate, the City was sickly encircled by its rat-infested slums. The Great Plague of London had fully earned its second name: the Poors' Plague.

Amos had gone to work at Lime House the week the rope walk closed. His crude efforts there gave him a feeling of high service, for London had a foulness that only caustic lime could cure.

Still wary of press gangs, he declined to be one of the carters who hauled limestone and shells from the docks to the kilns. All contacts with coal lighters he avoided, too. But as a fireman he must labor harder than the carters. There were sayings in England, long in use, which Amos and his fellow workers came to illustrate: "as red-faced as a lime-burner," "as thirsty as a limey." His skin became florid and dry; at times it blistered. He felt so parched that he could hardly get enough cool water to drink.

There was nothing inventive about Amos's work; merely a call for endurance. In the big cone-shaped kilns, fires must be kept constantly burning, those fires directly attacking the materials to be consumed. When the acid gases had been driven off by the blasting heat, limestone and shell were reduced to an alkaline powder. This was the precious and powerful quicklime so much in demand. It was drawn off in pans below the fire line, and every pound was spoken for. McTarvish, the foreman, would wring his hands and lament because they could not produce more of it. He would suffer acute stomach pains when the limestone barges were delayed and the kilns must mark time.

"Come and do your arithmetic, Skeet!" he would call from the old timbered office of Lime House. "No use wasting time!" And there at his littered desk he would compose sums for Amos to work, patient with the boy's mental slowness as he was never patient with his slowness of limb. "You've a good, slow mind, lad," he would say. "Once you grasp a thing, you possess it!"

Mrs. Skeet made a salve of mutton tallow and herbs for the protection of Amos's skin. Though it did not bleach him, it prevented blisters and soothed his eyelids. At Susan's suggestion he bought a pair of green spectacles, like those worn by Mr. Pepys on the water. He also bought a pair for a fellow lime-burner, who could not afford them because of his large family.

Amos was making unusually high wages now and, by October, was able to send his mother to Cheapside to buy herself a new outfit. Kip was sent with her to see that she bought nothing outlandish or of sleazy quality. Kip had a remarkable eye for women's clothes. He noticed them. He had always wanted to see his mother in a dark-green velvet dress and a beaver hat. This was out of the question on Amos's limited means, but he did pilot Mrs. Skeet to a green wool suit and hood that was very modish.

When Amos saw how neat and presentable their mother looked in her good new clothes, he decided to take her to call on Susan. He sent Kip to Navy Yard to ask Susan to set the time.

"Next Sunday!" Susan exclaimed without hesitating. "All of you come about two o'clock. Alice and I will have dinner for you."

Any decent company to break the tedium would have been welcome. That it was to be Amos and his family was a prospect almost too happy to be borne. She began to clean the house in a frenzy of industry. She inspected the larder anxiously, reconstructing the limited menu in every possible way. She frequently embraced Alice, to the latter's surprise and inconvenience. "Really, Suze!" Alice would shout impatiently; though she was glad enough they were to have guests to cook for. Her knitting was at a standstill because she had run out of yarn.

Amos was less concerned than Susan about the impending visit. Having weaned his parent from rum and supplied her with a new getup of clothes, even to gloves and a silk purse, he supposed he had nothing further to worry about. But he reckoned without Mrs. Skeet. No sooner had she laid eyes on Susan there in the Pepys doorway than she exclaimed:

"So this is the girl Amos has chose to be his mate! Let me have a look at ye, dearie!"

Susan glanced quickly at Amos, saw the dismay on his face, laughed. "No, Amos hasn't chosen me to be anything but a friend, Mrs. Skeet."

"Not his promised one? I do declare! He comes here so often, I thought he had intentions." Susan giggled; she could not help it, for Amos was so amazed at his mother. She welcomed them in.

"My, what a nice house!" said Mrs. Skeet. "It puts me in mind of my father's tavern at Brentwood; though it's more stacked up, you might say. My folks are gone from this world now, and strangers owns the tavern, but I still mind how it looked when I was a little child."

"The way I remember my grandfather's lodgings in Chancery Lane," Susan said. "He didn't own the house, but he leased the ground floor. I remember the cupboards there, where he stacked his books; and the tester bed my mother and I slept in; and the pigeon cote in the back yard."

"A person does remember," Mrs. Skeet responded gratefully. "Ye're right young to understand." She allowed Kip to divest her of the new coat, hat, and gloves, though reluctantly, for she was still dazed by the excitement of owning them.

Susan said, "I expect you'll want to keep your purse to get at your things?"

"So I will." Mrs. Skeet ate a horehound lozenge and wiped her nose on a lace-edged handkerchief to show that she was in every way equipped. Drawing the cords of her purse, she hung it on her arm and followed Susan to the dining room. "Amos says ye're a 'prentice girl here, dearie."

"Yes, Mrs. Skeet, I do all kinds of work, even to combing Mr. Pepys' wig. But mostly I help Alice, the cook. You'll meet her soon. She wears a patch over one eye and looks stern, but she's very good-humored and kind. Sit in the chair that has the pillows, Mrs. Skeet."

"Can I build up the fire for you, Susan?" Amos asked her.

"I'd be grateful if you would. Here's the tongs."

Amos built up a gay and leaping fire, having grown accustomed to that sort of thing at the kilns. Mr. Pepys would have shuddered to see how much coal he laid on.

Kip demanded to know what he could do to help.

"You can get the venison off the spit," Susan answered, and took him to the kitchen with her.

When they gathered at the table, Susan said grace; as the Skeets, all three, declined with the surprising explanation that they didn't know how; and Alice was too breathless.

The venison was a thing of wonder, and Susan watched

proudly while Alice carved it. Yesterday, miraculously, Mr. Pepys had sent half a haunch from the officers' mess, for he was on the Victualing Commission and could obtain it. He sent it boiled. Tom Edwards, when delivering it, warned that it must last them a week. But Susan and Alice, in a riotous fling of hospitality, elected to have it for the dinner party. To make it more appetizing, they had gashed it with herbs and subjected it to a second cooking, on the spit over charcoal.

"I've not smelled the like of it in years," Mrs. Skeet said. Kip hummed a tune. Amos held his flat stomach.

The other dishes, passed by Susan, were such foods as they had been able to get together: home-baked bread, dried peas, pickled cabbage, tea. Alice had provided the latter from her own private stock. For a sweet, they had apricot conserve on gingerbread.

When the venison had been reduced to a rich bone, Kip, in a hushed aside, bespoke it for his dog. Amos frowned, and Mrs. Skeet looked abashed, but Susan treated the request as a compliment. "If Alice is willing," she said, looking at Alice for permission.

"Why wouldn't I be!" Alice replied, for she saw that Susan wanted to commit this final folly, even if the soup kettle went bare. "We'll wrap up the bone for you to carry home, Kip."

Sitting before the dining-room fire after dinner, Mrs. Skeet could not be kept from rash pronouncements, though Amos tried his best to head her off. "Any girl that marries Amos will be welcome to live on our boat," she said, "as welcome as flowers in May." Receiving no answer, she continued, "Or, if she didn't fancy river life, her and Amos could set up in Stepney, in let lodgings."

Amos cleared his throat. Susan jumped up and swept the hearth. Kip and Alice waited expectantly, their eyes on Amos.

Amos knew it was hardly decent to talk of the plague at a party, but that was the dreadful straw he was forced to grasp. "Did young Mr. Montagu die of the plague?" he asked Susan, stopping his mother at last.

"No, he didn't die," Susan answered, "and it wasn't the plague he had. It turned out to be only smallpox. He and his family are staying with kinfolks at Dagenhams. They went there to be nearer Lord Montagu, while he's at sea, and that's where Sidney came down sick."

Kip asked the question that Amos wanted to ask. "Did his sister, Lady Anne, take the smallpox, too?"

"No. Only Sidney and a manservant, Mr. Pepys said."

"That's a piece of good luck!" Kip exclaimed. "Lady Anne's got such pretty skin."

Mrs. Skeet came back to her theme, a suitable mate for Amos. "Pretty skin," she said dreamily. "Yes, that's what all the girls want. They'll gather dew on a May Day, or they'll put buttermilk masks on their faces, just to get milky-white skin. But when Amos picks a wife, I hope he won't be misled by a satin cheek. Such a girl might lie abed of mornings, ne'er fixing 'im a packet o' food for his day's work. I'd rather Amos would find 'im a kind, sweet, mannerly girl that knows how to work." She looked at Susan Stokes thoughtfully and added, "If she's not fair-skinned and gold-haired, it needn't matter none."

Susan giggled and slyly winked at Amos. "Isn't your mother funny?" the wink said. "Isn't she cunning?"

Relieved, Amos grinned broadly. He knew his own need, and that need was supplied. If a chap is not ready to pledge himself to marry, he needs a girl who won't corner him.

For the next hour, Mrs. Skeet and Alice talked of herbs and spices and cooking. Mrs. Skeet remembered some tasty dishes from her father's ordinary, and she recited the rules to Alice until Alice had memorized them. Kip went about the room, examining things. Amos sat still and said almost nothing, but he was relaxed and strangely contented. Finally he said they must go home; and they made their grateful adieus and left, Kip carrying Singer's bone in an old parchment.

In the midst of washing the dishes, Susan said to Alice, meaning it, "Everything was perfect, wasn't it?"

"Why, yes, Suze. I ne'er saw a nicer party." Alice knew a girl in love when she saw one; widowed, herself, she remembered.

When Amos went again to Navy Yard he received a surprise, delivered by Alice. "Your girl's not here, Amos. She's gone down to Woolwich. Mrs. Pepys sent for 'er a-Thursday. She aimed to give a party in 'er lodgin's, and she needed Suze to cook the supper."

"Did Susan go by herself?" Amos asked.

"No, Mr. Pepys' clerk came to fetch 'er—Mr. Hewer, that is. He and Suze went loaded with extry dishes and the roastin' pan."

Amos was glad to hear that. If Susan had been escorted by Tom Edwards, the eighteen-year-old page, it would have been bothersome news. Edwards was always singing or strumming an instrument. He had been trained in the King's Choir. He could read well and hoped for a commission in the Navy. True, Susan said he ignored her because she worked in the kitchen, and she considered him "too conceited to live." But they might, speculated Amos, scratching his elbows there on the Pepys doorstep, have become a little congenial on a crowded barge to Woolwich.

"She'll be home a-Monday," Alice said. "Mr. Pepys promised me as much. I don't like to keep to this big house all by myself. There's money stored here. Ye know that, Amos."

"Yes, Susan told me. It's in an iron box in Mr. Pepys' closet. The box Susan tried her strength on."

This can best be explained by a statement in Mr. Pepys' diary, entered a year ago:

This day I received from Mr. Foley, but for me to pay for it, if I like it, an iron chest, having now received back some money I had laid out for the King, and I hope to have a good sum of money by me, thereby, in a few days, I think above 800 pounds. But when I came home at night, I could not find the way to open it; but which is a strange thing, my little girle Susan could carry it alone from one table clear from the ground

*and set upon another, when neither I nor anyone in my house
. . . could do it.*

Just before Susan Stokes performed this feat she had had a
brief illness that Mr. and Mrs. Pepys feared would turn out to
be measles or scarlet fever; but she failed to develop a rash and
was soon up and about. The truth was, Susan had a mild ague
that she had picked up in her childhood from living so near
Fleet Ditch. At certain seasons it would invade her blood; and
when the fever was on her, she had so much strength that she
surprised even herself. Afterward, when the fever was gone,
she would feel chilly and depleted for a few days, though she
never spoke of it.

Alice said, "Yes, that's the box, Amos. Pepys ought to put
his money with the goldsmiths, but he likes to keep it handy.
Sometimes I wonder how many sailors knows it's stored here!"

"Sailors are as honest as anybody!" Amos flared.

"I reckon sailors be as upright as shopkeepers and tailors,"
Alice apologized, "but some of 'em's in a bad way now. Those
that recover from the plague and still wear plasters on their
scars can't enlist again, nor they can't get work ashore. They
hang around Customhouse Dock and they come up Seethin'
Lane to Navy Yard, and sometimes they get to yellin',
'Where's the chest, Pepys? Where's the seamen's chest?'"

"Wait, now!" Amos said. "The thing they've got in mind is
the Seamen's Chest, spelled with big letters. It's a relief fund
for sailors, down at Chatham. Our dad used to hand over sixpence a month into it, out o' his sea pay."

Amos was right. The Chest had been started long ago by
Admirals Drake and Hawkins when everybody was grateful to
the sailors for defeating the Spaniards. But through the years
it had been so abused and neglected as to become a scandal.
Mr. Pepys was helping to reorganize it, to make it more useful
to sick and disabled sailors, but it was erroneous to suppose
that he kept the Chest moneys in his house.

"If they shout that way any more, Mrs. Alice," Amos said,
"tell 'em to go down to Chatham and see Commissioner Pett.

He's the one in charge of their fund. He allowed my mother six pounds. It wasn't near as much as our dad had paid in, but it helped."

Alice thanked Amos for his advice. She said she felt better, knowing the sailors were only shouting for their rights, not for Mr. Pepys' iron box. "But I'll be glad when Suze gets back, just the same," she said.

Like many a large woman of commanding appearance, Alice was not overly brave. Mr. Pepys knew this, but he had counted on her formidable looks when he left her in charge of his house during the plague. Standing in the open doorway, her arms akimbo, a towering cap on her head, she was impressive. When Amos thought of this forbidding woman relying on little Susan Stokes for courage, he had to laugh.

Several nights later Amos went again to the Pepys house, wanting to know if Susan had come home safely. She had and was considerably perked up from her trip. The supper had not been too difficult, she said, and she had been asked to join the dancing afterward. She had shared a sleeping room with Barbara Sheldon, the landlady's daughter; they had talked and giggled till daylight.

"Who brought you home today?" Amos asked her.

"Tom Edwards. Mr. Pepys sent him with some food for us."

"Did Edwards sing to you?" Amos asked.

"No. He was too busy sighing about his sweetheart. He's in love with Jane Gentleman, that lady's maid Mrs. Pepys had for a while."

"The one that lisped and was always blinking her green eyes."

"You remember her, I see. She's got several suitors, but I think she encourages Tom Edwards the most."

"It's a wonder you don't fall in love with Tom Edwards, yourself," Amos said sincerely. It was not in his nature to be sarcastic, and Susan knew it.

"Tom's just mad about Tom," she answered. "That's enough. If I fell in love with anybody in this house it would be with Mr. Hewer, for all that he's so old—twenty-five, if he's a day. But he hardly notices girls, and that's tiresome."

Put it down to fate that Susan Stokes would not become involved with those promising young men who frequented the same house with her. Tom Edwards would marry Jane Gentleman three years hence in a gay wedding paid for by Mr. and Mrs. Pepys. Will Hewer would fail to get the wife he aspired to; would remain a bachelor all his days, the stanch comfort of Mr. Pepys' declining years.

But to Amos that night, talking to Susan of the page and the clerk, something seemed to threaten. How could the three of them meet daily under the same roof without Susan's becoming desirable to the one or the other? And how could she fail to respond? And how could he, a lime-burner, beneath them all in birth, prevent it? And why should he want to prevent it if he didn't plan to marry Susan, himself? Was he like Aesop's animal, the dog in the manger? "Now I know what I am," he muttered.

Greatly disturbed, he bent to Susan and kissed her lips, not ardently but lingeringly. It was the kiss of a boy in search of himself. "Good night," he said gently, and put on his dusty cap and went away home.

Susan stood transfixed with joy. In the days that followed, the joy leveled to an abiding happiness that followed her to sleep and was with her like a bird song when she wakened.

Though Amos failed to return on the following Sunday, and she had no word from him, she was not disturbed.

A diversion occurred November twelfth, when Mrs. Pepys arrived suddenly at the house, accompanied by Mary, her haughty, handsome chambermaid. Both of them were smoldering and giving off sparks of anger. Mary went to the bedroom she shared with Mercer and there collected her clothes.

"Have you got all of them?" Mrs. Pepys asked, tapping the floor with her toe. "Every single thing?"

"Yes, I have," Mary answered in a composed, disdainful way.

"Even the ear pendants Mr. Pepys gave you?"

"I have those. Indeed, I have," replied Mary, tossing her head. She was never one to lose her temper, but poor Mrs. Pepys often lost hers. When Mary had departed in the hackney coach that was waiting, Mrs. Pepys wept aloud and walked the floor, putting on a very fine act for Alice and Susan.

"She's going to stay with Mrs. Pierce!" she wailed. "She'll tell Mrs. Pierce everything!"

Mrs. Pierce, a pretty woman admired by Mr. Pepys, was the popular and frivolous wife of one James Pierce, surgeon to the Duke of York. Mrs. Pepys had indiscreetly called her a "crooked gallant" and an "overdressed jade" in the presence of Mary; she had really pulled Mrs. Pierce's reputation to shreds. And now Mary was going to be Mrs. Pierce's personal maid, and they would pull Mrs. Pepys to shreds in return. They would discuss her jealousy, and laugh about it. They would titter about her studying music when she had no talent but only wanted to be praised by her husband. They would tell that she hadn't had a pound of dowry when Pepys married her, for all that she had been to a French convent school and was so mannerly. And they would say openly, for all to hear, that Sam Pepys had never given his wife that string of pearls he had promised her.

Mrs. Pepys' tension increased as she thought how she was at the mercy of those gossips. "Anyway, I detest Sam, so what does it matter?" she stormed. In her frustration, she butted her head against the chimney piece, like a child.

Susan ran for smelling salts and applied them. Alice led the distraught creature to a chair and bathed her face in cold water. "No, now," Alice comforted, her stern face gone tender, "ye don't mean what ye say. Hush up, do! Ye're shakin' yourself to pieces. Everybody's got their troubles, and some's worse than yours."

Susan too had become excited. "Poor Mrs. Pepys!" she exclaimed, "you've raised a bump on your forehead! I'll get the arnica! It's in the kitchen cupboard."

After a while Mrs. Pepys was soothed. She asked Susan to go upstairs and find her beaver hat and yellow petticoat and bring them down. She needed to take them with her because Mrs. Penn was having a party at Woolwich that night.

Alice accompanied her mistress down Seething Lane to Tower Wharf, carrying the hatbox and begging her to be calm and to forego malice for the sake of her health.

As Elizabeth Pepys was about to take barge, she impulsively kissed Alice's hand, though one was not supposed to do such a thing in plague time. "I've often been mean to you, Alice," she said contritely. "To Susan too. Though neither of you has ever tried to lure my husband away from me, the way some have."

"Lor'!" Alice exclaimed, surprised. "What would I want with 'im? And Suze wants only Amos Skeet!"

Susan, lying in bed that night in the room she shared with Alice, could not go to sleep. It was not because of Alice's snoring, for she was used to that. It was because the Pepys marriage was so disillusioning. She faced the facts that Mr. Pepys was an indifferent husband, and that Mrs. Pepys repaid him by being a shrew. How had it all started? With Mr. Pepys, surely; for he put his pleasures before everything else. That was the sort of man Elizabeth St. Michel had drawn in the lottery of marriage when she was too young to know better. It could happen to anyone who married hastily, Susan reasoned. Though Mrs. Pepys had been starry-eyed and devoted, Susan's thoughts raced on, her husband had soon begun to neglect her. And now he bought ear pendants for chambermaids, and dashed from supper party to supper party, and kissed other women behind doors, and gave them kid gloves and silk hose at St. Valentine's.

Susan tried to picture herself and Amos in this situation; but the picture seemed absurd, and she giggled. Amos would have to use salt herring for gifts, which would be comical.

Then, serious again, she remembered something Mrs. Pepys had told her a fortnight ago in Woolwich. They had been preparing apples to bake, peeling and quartering them and adding spices.

"I learned to peel and core fruit when I was first married," Elizabeth Pepys confided to Susan. "Sam and I couldn't afford to dine at taverns then. We would carry our food home from the greengrocer's and the butcher's, and I'd cook it in our attic fireplace. We had only one tablecloth to our names. But those were the happiest days of my whole life."

This conversation came back to Susan right pleasantly. It reminded her that love can abide in garrets; that silken curtains are not needed to keep love from flying out the window.

Alice gave a mighty snort, came half awake, sensed Susan's wakefulness. "Light a candle and read if you want to, Suze," she mumbled kindly, then slept again.

But Susan wanted only to think; she was about to get hold of something. She reflected that Mr. and Mrs. Pepys still loved each other. But money-getting and social ambition and madcap friends had got in the way. When a young couple is poor, she thought to herself there in the dark, they have to pull together; it's the best way, I think. . . . Though I'd not want to be poverty-rid. I'd suffer to see my little children go hungry and dirty. I'd want us to strive and get ahead, Amos and me. . . . But poor people hardly ever get ahead in London, I notice, unless they've got rich kin to advance them. Might it be different in New England, as Mr. Pepys calls that place, if a family can get there?

She fell asleep wondering, but not happily. Like a minor melody was the recollection that Amos's dream of America had come to him because of another girl, not herself.

The plague had lessened in London, and some of the braver exiles were returning.

Mrs. Pepys, wanting her home like any housewife, came to it in December. But Mr. Pepys must remain a while longer at Navy headquarters in Greenwich. Mrs. Pepys wore herself out, taking barge to Greenwich to join him at parties and coming

home next day to rest her aching head. Mercer accompanied
her to and fro, and those two often clashed. Mercer was paid
to be a companion, and when Mrs. Pepys tried to induce her
to be a lady's maid or a chambermaid, replacing Mary, Mercer
would revolt. Then Susan must leave the housework and rush
upstairs and do Mrs. Pepys' hair, or whatever lacked.

Another trial was the frequent preparation of oysters for
Mr. Pepys' stag parties. He would dispatch them by the barrel
for Susan and Alice to shuck for him. And once Mrs. Pepys,
coming up from Woolwich in a hired coach, brought three
huge turkeys for them to kill and pluck and dress.

When Mr. Pepys came home to stay in January, the pace
quickened. He was a member of several commissions now—
the Navy could hardly whip a cat, it was said, but Pepys must
hold its tail—and he had made new merchant friends who
dropped in for meals. Among those were the Houblon brothers, who sent their own ships to sea. If Pepys stood in his
kitchen door and told Alice and Susan that the Houblons were
coming to dinner, he meant all five of them. Pepys was also,
nowadays, close to the Duke of York at Whitehall Palace.
For his interviews with the Duke he wanted his fine shirts
and vests kept pressed, his new wig combed. Besides all these
high and mighty demands, he wanted his silver cups and dishes
polished frequently, and his wainscot scrubbed every week. As
the three upper servants were too high for those tasks—Will
Hewer and Mercer and Tom Edwards—all devolved upon Susan and Alice. To get help from the others, they must plead
for it.

During that hard winter, Amos Skeet came whenever he
could to see Susan, going to the kitchen door where he knew
he would find her. He was working now on Sundays as well as
weekdays, for the plague's slow abatement was bringing a final
desperate call for quicklime. Amos was always very thin, very
tired, very dusty when he came. His feet would be dragging.
His eyes would be red-rimmed and hollow. Susan, hearing his
whistle as she washed the supper dishes, would stop with ex-

clamations of pleasure, would get him supper and make him eat it at the deal table. Then, all too soon, he would trudge homeward in the frosty night, and Susan would wonder if she had dreamed his presence.

Kip's visits were more natural. He came during the daytime and he was himself. The plague had not made him meek or cautious, and he still threw stones when out delivering fish. He would tell Susan of encounters he had had with some objectionable boys in Wapping, or with tippling dock hands. And once he boasted of seeing his well-remembered enemies, the two fishwives, and peppering them with pebbles as they were delivering fish in Aldersgate Street.

"What were you doing there, yourself?" Susan asked pointedly.

Amos had told her that Kip had taken to wandering the streets north of the City. "Let him get a little spare time," Amos had said, "and off he goes, following Hound's Ditch around the Wall. I don't know who his friends are. He never says, and I've not got time to pump it out of 'im."

With this information in mind, Susan repeated her question in different words. "Do you have friends in Aldersgate Street, Kip?"

"Yes, I have," Kip answered showily. "A gang of 'em."

That was a word Mr. Pepys sometimes used, but Susan was not sure of its meaning. "That gang of Albemarle's," Pepys sometimes said. He also spoke of "the French gang," and of "Lord Berkeley's gang," and always in critical tones. Kip, however, had conveyed admiration when he used the term.

"Do you ever go to the homes of your new friends, Kip?"

"Sometimes I do. They've got good places to live, better'n mine. They treat me fine any time I drop around. I help 'em move goods when they need me to."

"What do you mean by that? What sort of goods?"

"Clothes, mostly. And last week we carried furniture to a man's house in Chiswell Street. I got paid two shilling sixpence."

"That's nice," Susan said, impressed. "Did you tell your mother and Amos about it?"

"I told Muv. Amos is too tired to listen any more. Say, Suze, have you got a bone for Singer?"

Susan had. She also had a small cheesecake for Mrs. Skeet; she had put it aside from yesterday's baking. "How's your mother getting along?" she asked Kip. "Does she stay well?"

"She's well, I reckon. But—" He hesitated.

"But what, Kip? What's wrong?"

"The plague makes her sad. Three of her friends has died of it this winter. She went to the buryin's at Stepney after Amos told her not to go. When she come home from the last one— came home," he corrected himself, eying Susan, "she said she'd feel better if she had a little hot rum. So I took some money I had and bought her a half bottle of rum from a sailor at Wapping. I mixed her some in a mug with hot water and lemon, the way she told me to, and sure 'nuff it helped 'er. She dropped off to sleep, and I went to Lime House to see if there was any work for me. When me and Amos come home—came home— that night, we saw she wasn't herself. She had woke up and finished the bottle. Amos cuffed me hard. He raised a knot on my jaw."

"Oh, mercy," Susan said. "When did this happen?"

Kip counted back. "It was Wednesday, three days agone. I've learnt my lesson." He felt his jawbone ruefully.

"I hope so. You meant to be kind, but it was the wrong thing to do. It made a lot of worry for Amos. Has your mother been depressed since it happened?"

"What's that?"

"Has she been downhearted more than natural?"

"She has, for a fact. She cries and moans and stays on her bunk. 'Let the plague carry me off,' she keeps sayin'. 'All my friends is dead, and my boys begrudge me a little rum.' That's the way she goes on. I'm pretty tired of it."

"I'd think you would be! It's a useless way for her to act. She's just piling trouble on Amos."

Thus Susan, with the arrogance of youth, passed judgment on poor Mrs. Skeet. She put the cheesecake and the beef bone into a willow basket and gave them to Kip as he put on his cap for departure. "And here's a handkerchief I hemmed for you," she said.

He thanked her warmly for everything. "I'll be back Monday or Tuesday," he said, "unless I go to Aldersgate Street."

"Go there, if you can pick up some more work, Kip. That two shilling sixpence was good pay for a boy your age."

Thus Susan's youth and ignorance spoke again. The work she advised Kip to pursue was part of a youthful crime trend. It would presently surprise the judges of the Sessions Court at Old Bailey Prison, and those men were not easily surprised.

One day toward the end of March, Mrs. Pepys brought from Westminster in a hackney coach a young woman with luggage. Susan opened the door for them and was pleased to see that Mrs. Pepys had fetched green-eyed Jane, her former personal maid. Now Mrs. Pepys would have someone to dress her, to hang up her clothes, and make the beds. What a relief! Susan hurried to the kitchen to break the news to Alice.

"Glory be!" Alice exclaimed. "I've heard Mrs. Pepys brag of Jane's cooking, many's the time. Now I can quit."

"No, Alice," Susan said hastily. "You're mixed up. They've had two cooks named Jane, but this is not either one of 'em. It's Jane Gentleman, a lady's maid they used to have. She stays clear of the kitchen. She can't cook at all."

"Then let 'er learn!" Alice said. "My sister needs me in Islington, and blood's thicker than water. Ye very well know, Suze, I've only stayed the winter here for your sake. But now I'll be off. I'm wore out with these daffy folk."

And so Mr. Pepys wrote morosely in his journal next day:

Up and away goes Alice, our cook-mayde, a good servant, whom we loved . . . after having given her mistress warning fickly for a quarter of a year.

Now, indeed, came the hard days for Susan. She had become chief cook overnight, with none to help her in the kitchen; with six adults to cook for, besides herself.

Mr. and Mrs. Pepys, in their casual ways, tried to remedy this, as a diary entry three weeks later shows:

The plague, I hear, encreases in the town much, and exceedingly in the country everywhere. Away home, on my way asking in two or three places the worth of pearls, I being now come to the time that I have long ago promised my wife a necklace. My wife and I and the girl [Jane] by coach to Islington, and there eat and drank in the coach and so home, and there find a girle sent at my desire by Mrs. Mitchell of Westminster Hall, to be my girle under the cooke-mayde, Susan. But I am a little dissatisfied that the girle, though young, is taller and bigger than Su, and will not, I fear, be under her command, which will trouble me. So to my accounts and journal, there being bonfires in the streete for St. George's Day.

Next day he reported indifferently:

April 24th. Up, and presently am told that the girle that came yesterday has packed up her things to be gone home again to Enfield, whence she came, which I was glad of. The reason was that London do not agree with her. So I did give her something, and away she went.

But Susan was not glad. "Try it a while, Judith," she had begged the girl. "I'll show you how they like things done here, and I'll ask Mrs. Pepys to let you go home every week's end, if you crave it. Do give the place a try!"

But the girl, already homesick for Enfield village, could not be persuaded. The sight of the Tower of London frightened her, and so did the sound of the bells, tolling for funerals. "London's a drear place," she said, strapping shut her cloak bag. "At home, the apple orchard's in bloom. Here, all's ugly."

She was not a slut, but a well-bred country girl, cousin to Mrs. Mitchell who had a bookstall in Westminster Hall. Susan watched a hackney coach take her away. For the first time she realized how much she longed for a companion of her own age and sex. She sat at the kitchen table and wept rebelliously.

Yet the climax had not been reached. A new burden of work was in store for her. Mr. Pepys had just had banisters built around his "leads," transforming that retreat into an outdoor dining room; though to reach it from the kitchen, a servant must traverse the lower floor, ascend the parlor stairs, traverse the second floor, and step out of a french window in the Pepys bedroom. The night after Judith departed, Mr. Pepys wrote proudly:

So home, and with my wife and Mercer spent our evening upon our new leads by our bedchamber, singing, while Mrs. Mary Batelier looked out of the window to us, and we talked together. My wife and I staid there till eleven o'clock at night, and it is a convenience I would not want for anything in the world, it being, methinks, better than almost any roome in my house. So, having supped upon the leads, to bed. The plague, blessed be God! is decreased sixteen this week.

Susan had served Will Hewer and Tom Edwards and Jane Gentleman in the dining room before carrying supper to Mr. and Mrs. Pepys and Mercer under the stars. Fortunately, Jane and Tom offered to go upstairs to the roof and bring down the supper dishes. They were renewing their romance, finding every opportunity to be together. This gave them a chance to rub shoulders on the stairs.

"Oh, I do thank you!" Susan exclaimed when they brought the trays to the kitchen.

"It was nothing," Jane said, smiling brightly.

Tom made a careless salute, not interrupting a song he was singing. They went out of the room together, hand and hand, without offering to help with the dishes. Susan shrugged. Some girls had their sweethearts near them, she thought glumly; under the very roof with them; but others must be forever deprived. Could she, Susan Stokes, even be sure she had a sweetheart? She had not seen Amos for several weeks, nor had Kip come to bring any news of him.

On Sunday Mr. Pepys put in a full day. He went to Morning Prayer at St. Olave's. After dinner—which Susan served on the run—he went by water to Redriffe, accompanied by Tom Edwards, and thence walked to Mr. John Evelyn's place at Deptford—an estate called Sayes Court. Greatly refreshed by contact with Mr. Evelyn's fine mind and by the beauty of his formal garden, Pepys picked up his page at Redriffe and returned home . . .

Where [says his journal entry] *I find my uncle and aunt Wight, and supped with them upon my leads with mighty pleasure and mirth, and they being gone, I mighty weary to bed . . . it being mighty hot weather.*

If Mr. Pepys could misuse the word *mighty*, so could Susan. As she was undressing that night she exclaimed to herself in an angry voice, "I'm mighty tired of being a slave in this house!" And she hurled both her shoes against the wall.

Jane and Tom, hearing her as they passed the door, laughed. Jane said, "The Pepyses had better hurry and get a second cook! Susan's showing some temper."

Susan endured the hardships of the next two days without another outburst and without faltering. But on Wednesday she told Mrs. Pepys she felt the need of lying down. "My head aches," she confessed, "and my back feels queer. Every time I bend over, I want to holler."

"Do go to bed, then, Susan," Mrs. Pepys said. "Stay there till tomorrow morning. We'll manage supper without you."

And so Mr. Pepys wrote in his journal that evening:

My wife tells me the ill news that our Susan is sicke and gone to bed, with great pain in her head and back, which troubles us all.

It was May Day, a time when a girl should be in a country meadow, gathering dew for her complexion. Susan thought of this as she lay in bed, and she laughed wildly. She had been chilly, but now she was hot with fever. Daylight turned to twilight; twilight merged with darkness. Once in the night Susan called loudly for Alice, forgetting that Alice was gone.

But, on the whole, the long rest in bed restored her strength, and when morning came she got up and began the day's ordeal. It could never be said of Susan Stokes that she gave up easily. She made no complaint, and, though her color was bad, Mr. and Mrs. Pepys supposed that she was recovering.

But the following morning, she could not get up at all. When Tom Edwards knocked on her door and asked, "Where's breakfast, Susan?" her only reply was, "Go 'way!"

"I reckon Susan's feeling worse," the page said to Mr. Pepys. "She refuses to get up."

"Another day in bed won't hurt her," Pepys replied. "I dare say we've overworked her since Alice quit."

Mrs. Pepys, hearing the news, went to investigate. She felt Susan's forehead in a gingerly way and retreated across the room. "Let me bring you a waiter of food," she said. "You'll feel better if you eat something."

"Not now," Susan begged. "Let me alone." She knew Mrs. Pepys was thinking of the plague or the smallpox, but she did not share her alarm. It was her old fever, she suspected; only worse this time because she was so weary. Turning her face to the wall, she drifted into semiconsciousness.

Mrs. Pepys, baffled, went out and shut the door. Looking into the kitchen, she saw that it was in great disorder. Mr. Pepys and Tom had gotten their own breakfasts with masculine carelessness and had not bothered to stack the dirty dishes. An egg was broken on the flagstone floor. There was a smell of stale beer. The fire had gone out in the stove, and the charcoal bin was empty.

Elizabeth Pepys threw up her hands and went to her easel in the parlor. Her painting master, Mr. Browne, was due at ten. He had instructed her to paint a bowl of fruit for him, and she had not completed it. He might refuse to bother with her if she failed his assignments. He was a slender, handsome, impatient young man with tapering fingers and a tapering nose. Sometimes he complimented her. She would ask him to stay for dinner, she decided. But first she must waken Mercer and Jane and ask them to set the house straight.

She went to the foot of the stair well and called them awake. "Do get up!" she cried urgently. "Susan's sick and can't do her work! Susan's sick in bed!"

Mr. Pepys' diary tells the outcome of that day:

May 3rd. Up, and all the morning at the office. At noon home and contrary to my expectation find my little girle Su worse than she was, which troubled me, and the more to see my wife minding her paynting and not thinking of her house business. . . . I was angry with my wife and would not have Browne to think to dine at my table with me always, being desirous to have my house to myself without a stranger. . . . Upon this my wife and I had a little disagreement, but it ended by and by, and then to send up and down for a nurse to take the girle home, and would have given anything. . . . Sent for the girle's mother; she came and undertakes to get her daughter a lodging and nurse at next doore to her, though she dare not, for the parish's sake, whose sexton her husband is, to have her into her owne house. Thence home, calling at my bookseller's and other trifling places, and in the evening the mother came and with a nurse she has got, who demanded, and I did agree to pay, at 10 shillings per weeks to take her, and so she away, and my house mighty uncouth, having so few in it.

Please to leave Susan Stokes a while to her misery, for Mr. Pepys will not mention her again for some days.

Amos too had run out of luck, but he forbade Kip to take the news to Susan, and so there occurred a loss of contact.

Amos had collapsed at work one day and was brought home on a litter by two laborers. Mr. Nokes, seeing them approaching the dock, halted them.

"If it's plague," he called, "don't come nigh the wharf! Take him to the Stepney pesthouse!"

The men who bore the litter said it was a heat stroke and nothing more. As the argument mounted, Mrs. Skeet darted from the houseboat and ran to her son's assistance. Looking at Amos and feeling his skin, she agreed with the carriers.

"Carry the boy to our boat there," she instructed, "and lay 'im on his bunk. Get 'im out of the sun, quick as you can." As for the dock owner, she shook a stern finger at him. "Shame on ye, Nokes!" she cried. "This boy has wore himself out, makin' quicklime! For that, would ye send 'im to a pesthouse to catch the disease ye're so afeard of?"

Mr. Nokes had the grace to say, "Sorry," and to let them pass.

And so Amos lay as helpless as he had lain once before. The first time, cold water had done him in; this time, it was flame and smoke. The fires of the limekilns had taken so much moisture from his skin and organs that he was like a person parched by a tropical sun. His eyes were seriously affected. Bloodshot, they pained him until he could not endure the light of day.

Kip was much troubled to see his strong, elder brother so weakened. His concern took a practical turn; he waited on Amos's every need. He busied himself, too, in scrubbing the houseboat and in delivering fish as promptly as his mother could cure them.

Early one Sunday afternoon, seeing Amos asleep, Kip told Mrs. Skeet that he would like to go to see his new friends in Aldersgate Street.

"Go, then," she said. "Ye deserve a bit o' fun. But be home before dark or I'll switch your legs, old as ye be."

"Oh, Muv!" Kip said in disgust. He could not imagine standing still and letting his mother thrash his legs, as she used to do when he was younger. He was almost fourteen years old now, rather short for his years, and for that reason all the more determined to be his age.

After taking Singer for a walk and tethering him again on deck, Kip put on a cap and coat of Amos's and went ashore.

"Why would ye wear a coat on such a warm day?" Mrs. Skeet shouted after him. "And if ye must, why not your own?"

Kip walked on. "Good-by, Muv," he said, and mumbled as if giving an answer. It was a way he had when he needed to evade.

Kip hurried through Whitechapel and followed Hound's Ditch—a respectable wagon road, in spite of its name—to Moorfields. Here he loitered at the courtyard of Bedlam, some sprawling buildings once known as the Priory of Bethlehem, forever dedicated to the care of the insane. Formerly, the mind-sick inmates had been gently cared for by nuns. But now, under the City, a more severe treatment was used; chained wrists and ankles were an almost uniform condition. Some of the sick ones made a terrible clamor. Others stood or crouched silently in the barred courtyard, their faces vacant. These seemed to have no wants or needs.

Kip was looking for a particular inmate, a person whom he had seen once before; an unchained man with good features and gentle brown eyes who somehow managed to keep himself clean. Kip had got to talking to him one day last month when he was passing, and the man had asked him for the core of an apple he was eating.

"I like apples," the fellow had said. "Save me your core. I used to have a whole tree o' apples nigh to my back door."

Kip immediately left off crunching his apple and handed it through the barred fence. Then he questioned the pitiful beggar. Right listlessly the man replied that his name was Nath Sunday, that he had been locked up in Bedlam for sorcery.

"Is that witchcraft?" Kip wanted to know.

"Yes. All my neighbors' kine died, out around Tottenham. It was a sickness the cows had, but they laid it to me. I'd not take oath for myself in court, for I'm one of the Fanatics— Quakers, they call us, because, now and again, we shake with rapture. Oath-taking is against our faith. That suited my brother. He testified against me and had me put away here. Now he's got my house and fields. He's got the apple tree I spoke of, and all my clothes."

"Your own brother would do that to you?" Kip was amazed. He thought of himself and Amos and the love they bore each other.

"But I bear him no hatred, mind ye. Therein would be sin."

"Why don't you wear chains, like the others here?"

"Because there's no need, ye see, and they know it. I do jobs here. I repair the crumbling stone walls. I lay the tiles. They couldn't use me, fettered."

"You might walk away sometime, when a gate's opened."

"I've got no clothes but these Bedlam rags that mark a man. I'd be o'ertaken and brought back."

"I'll bring you a coat, next time I come," Kip promised rashly. . . . And today he had remembered that promise and had worn an old coat and cap of Amos's, and was prepared to part with them if he should see the man.

He saw him. The inmate was standing where he had stood before, looking out and scanning the passers-by. Seeing Kip, his gentle face lit up with recognition. Kip began to remove the coat and cap he wore, pretending he found them too warm —as indeed he did—and sauntered to the high iron fence. Many persons were loitering on the pavements and peering into the courtyard. Some guffawed and threw trash at the inmates, for it was common practice to taunt the demented and make them rage and curse.

Kip pushed the coat and cap through the fence, and the man's callused hands grasped them avidly. "They belong to my brother," Kip said in a low voice. "My name's Kip Skeet. We live at Dick's Shore in a houseboat. Here's fourpence for you. I wish you well, Mr. Sunday."

"Ye're a good boy. Don't ever let man or law tell ye otherwise. Do ye know where I might find work?"

"I do, for a fact, if you're not afraid of the plague."

"A Bedlam man fears nothing, boy. Say where."

"Go to the church in Stepney and tell the parish clerk you'll help bury the dead. They need gravediggers real bad. They'll not mind hirin' a Fanatic, I reckon. Can you make it out o' here today?"

"I can try in about an hour. This is Easter Day. When the chaplains and the visitors leave, I'll go out amongst 'em, God willing. Be on your way now, boy. Don't involve yourself further."

Kip went off in the direction of Moorsgate. Looking back, he saw Nath Sunday put on the coat and cap and move toward the big gate of Bedlam's courtyard.

Kip felt very happy. His heart was alight with a warm glow for having helped a fellow human. He had often gotten the glow when helping animals too, but never to such an extent as this. Because of his efforts, an innocent man would escape the horrors of Bedlam and would walk free.

If only Kip had ended his day's adventures thus! But he had something else in mind—an encounter with his interesting new acquaintances. And so he went to Aldersgate Street, a wide and decent thoroughfare outside the Wall, running northward from the City toward Islington.

On a corner in an excellent neighborhood—a place known to him—he found three half-grown youths and a younger boy, conferring. The latter was not more than twelve years old, and Kip knew him as Little Parker. He knew the oldest boy as Kobet, the acknowledged leader; and a third boy was known to him by his surname of Mordant. The fourth, he had never seen before.

"Halloo, Skeet!" Kobet called, and he drew a circle in the air with the forefinger of his right hand, clockwise. The other boys duplicated his gesture.

"Halloo, Kobet, and the rest of you," Kip replied, and he drew some dashing circles in the air, himself, as many circles as there were boys. He had feared they had forgotten him, for it was all of a month since their last meeting. He had never known why they took him on, in the first place, and the wonder of it was still with him. He had been sauntering past this corner one day, and they had eyed him; and Kobet had stepped out and offered him a job. "Would you like to help us carry a chest of clothes?" That was the way it started.

But now, several of those boys were missing; and in their stead was a new boy who, to Kip's surprise, was called Montagu. "Skeet, shake hands with Montagu," Kobet said; and Kip did so, greatly impressed.

"Come on to my place," Montagu invited them all, and led them to the stable of his father's town house in a street bisecting Aldersgate. He took them into a coach room, all but filled by a large and ornate carriage. Some shelves had been built along one wall, and here were mugs and brierwood pipes, as in a real tavern. Tobacco and ale were available under the shelf.

"Help yourselves," Montagu invited.

"I might just try the snuff," Kip offered.

"Do, old chap," Montagu said, and watched indifferently while Kip took a pinch and placed it under his tongue. When he gagged and coughed, they all laughed.

"Ale?" asked Montagu.

"No," Kip answered. "Ale don't agree with me. It bloats me."

"It bloats me too," Little Parker said, giving Kip a grateful look. Kip thought him a very decent sort.

"Say, Montagu," Kip exclaimed, "are you kin to Lady Anne Montagu, the one that her father's an admiral?"

"We're cousins. My father's James, third son of the Earl of Manchester."

"Oh." Kip wanted to say that Lady Anne Montagu had once kissed his brother Amos in the Pepys back yard, but it seemed unsuitable, and he held his tongue.

Montagu poured ale for himself and Mordant and Kobet.

Mordant was of the same pattern as Montagu. They were about fifteen years old, pale, aristocratic, pimply, and dispirited. In afteryears Kip, recalling them, would hardly be able to separate Mordant from Montagu. Having been pampered all their lives and waited on by servants, they did not know how to fill the long hours of a day. They must have felt pitifully useless and lost, just waiting to grow up, not needed by their fashionable families. They were prey to boredom.

Kobet, on the other hand, was a brutal-looking youth with high color, coarse features, and an excess of vitality. He was the son of a successful tallow chandler, a man of force who had bothered to give his son but one piece of advice, "Get ahead."

"Kobet's seventeen years old," Little Parker whispered to Kip.

"I've got a brother almost eighteen," Kip boasted in reply. But, as always, he was excited by Kobet's swashbuckling ways. He saw that even on Montagu premises, Kobet held the reins.

Montagu again poured ale, and the three drank up. Kip wondered if they would soon be staggering. He nudged Parker in the ribs and muttered, "They'll be sick, sure as blazes."

Kobet told several remarkable tales. In all of them he played the leading role, the role of a young man who could get money without working for it. He explained that sometimes he did this by pretending to be deaf, dumb, and needy; sometimes by feigning to be a foreigner who had lost his purse and his directions. In every case he managed to have an amusing time and a loan of money from some kindhearted fool.

Listening to Kobet, Kip wondered how he, Kip Skeet, could have thought it so fine and exciting an hour ago to slip a coat and cap to a stupid Quaker in Bedlam.

The three older boys wore watches in their pockets and frequently consulted them. Once Kobet said, "What's holding things up, I wonder?"

"What does he mean?" Kip whispered to Little Parker.

"How should I know?" Little Parker answered. He and

Kip were withdrawn from the others, sitting on the carriage tongue. "It's some plan of Kobet's. It'll make us famous, is all I know. It'll put us ahead of the Shambles gang."

"Why did they take on a boy as young as you?" Kip asked in a practical turn of mind.

"I carry messages for Kobet, like telling the gang where to meet. I'm a pretty fast runner."

"Where do you live?" Kip whispered.

"Right near here. We've got a buttery full of food. I bring rations for the gang, and we store it in a house in Chiswell Street."

"Do you mean where we carried the big chest of clothes that day last fall? And the furniture last month?"

"Yes, that's the place."

As Kip was feeling empty, his mind reverted to the food. "What sort of vittles do you bring for the gang?"

"Hams and cheese and bacon—stuff like that."

"Don't your mother miss it?"

"She never goes to that part of the house."

"Oh," Kip said, "you're rich people."

Little Parker considered. "I reckon we're well off."

"Do you know something?" Kip said. "I'll bet somebody gets blamed for liftin' those cheeses and smoked meats out o' your house."

"You mean a servant, maybe? That'd be foul, wouldn't it?"

"Yes. You take my brother and me. We've got a good friend that's a servant in Navy Yard. She's a 'prentice cook, a real nice girl named Susan. We'd hate like thunder to see *her* get blamed in a deal like that."

Little Parker nodded, looking unhappy and confused.

Kobet began to tell another story, and they listened. It concerned the way to avoid paying hackney fare: pretend to lose your purse, berate the coachman, and walk away. While Montagu was questioning him about the fine points of this trick, the air was rent with cries of "Fire!"

"Come on!" Kobet said, and dashed outdoors. They followed

him. Though no smoke or flames were visible, he seemed to know the fire's location to be northward and headed for it like a sprinter.

"He's got a good nose," Kip panted as he and Little Parker strove to keep up.

Several blocks up Aldersgate Street, where the dwellings had become commercial, the boys arrived at the house that was afire. On its premises there was a public cockpit, and here, amid the straw, the fire had started. Now it was attacking the main building, a tavern of some size.

From the nearest well, water was being pumped by a fire engine, manned by sweating volunteers. Two lines of bucket brigades operated between the engine and the burning buildings. Crowds of curious persons cluttered the grounds, more hindrance than help.

Kobet studied the situation for a few minutes and then issued orders to his four followers. He told Montagu and Mordant where to stand: just below two windows on the side of the tavern farthest from the smoke. Then he ordered Kip and Little Parker to come with him. "We must save what's worth saving," he declared in a noble tone of voice.

As in most hostels, steep stairways abounded. Kip and Parker followed Kobet up a rather secluded one and arrived at the deserted second floor.

The quarter-hour that followed was like a dream to Kip, an exhilarating dream in which he played a hero's part. He and Kobet and Little Parker gathered up whatever objects were lying loose and dropped them out of the windows to Montagu and Mordant. They fell into an herb bed, no doubt the pride of the innkeeper's wife, and so escaped injury. As fast as things fell, Montagu and Mordant put them into pushcarts that had miraculously appeared just in the nick of time. Two little boys operated the carts and trundled the salvaged property away.

"Where are they taking the stuff?" Kip asked, panting from exertion and excitement.

"Where it'll be safe," Kobet answered in a short way. "Come now, step lively. We've got a few more rooms to do."

"I hear other people moving around up here," Kip said hopefully. But Kobet did not seem cheered by the news. Kip was filled with admiration to realize that their leader preferred to do this salvage work without adult help.

Kobet continued to go through cupboards and drawers in the tavern bedrooms, and in most cases he found them empty, the occupants having carried off what they could on departing. But, now and then, Kobet would find in a drawer a watch that had been overlooked, or some silver buckles, or a gold ring; these, he would drop into his pocket. However, such plunder as pewter pitchers and basins, rugs, comforters, footstools, candlesticks, and abandoned boots and clothing he ordered flung out the windows.

Little Parker, coughing from the smoke, made a protest. "I'm pretty tired of this. If the owners can't save their own stuff, let it burn!"

"That's the way with runts," Kobet answered severely, "always getting tired. If you must quit, carry this little piece of furniture downstairs with you. It's a fine game table, inlaid. Tell Montagu and Mordant to take special care of it."

"All right," Little Parker said, and he went down the staircase which they had ascended, lugging his burden and coughing.

Kip remained, being ashamed to do otherwise, for it was evident that Kobet despised a quitter. But he slacked his efforts, and he commenced to speculate as to what they were doing there. Could it be that Kobet was up to no good? It looked queer, now that he came to think of it. And how about those other times he had helped Kobet move things? Where had the property come from?

Kobet saw Kip looking at him strangely. "We've done the best we could, Skeet," he said suddenly. "Suppose we go?" And he was out of the room and down the stairs before Kip could reply. His hands were empty, his footfall noiseless. Kip went down more noisily, for he could not control his clumsy shoes; and he carried a little book with a leather cover, not wanting to let it burn.

Outdoors again, Kip saw Kobet conferring with a person he recognized. It was the man who had received the clothing and furniture in Chiswell Street. He was not yet middle-aged, but he was dissipated in looks and had an irritable manner. Well dressed and self-assured, he had the air of a man who moved in society. Kip recalled that he bore the good London name of Gabriel Holmes.

Seeing Kip watching them, Kobet and the mysterious Holmes moved away together, into the crowd.

Kip could not locate Montagu or Mordant, or any of the salvaged property that had been dropped from the windows; the herb bed was trampled and empty. Little Parker too had disappeared.

Kip was diverted by some shouts from the bucket carriers. The engine had suddenly failed in pumping water, though the well was not yet empty. Kip went as close to the disturbance as he could get, and he listened to the various theories as to the cause of the water failure. Presently it was discovered that a plug had been pulled from the engine, and all the water, so hard got from the well, was running out onto the ground.

"This looks strange!" exclaimed an imposing man who wore a gold chain of office around his neck. He was Sir Joseph Sheldon, one of London's two sheriffs. He said it was evident that the engine had been tampered with; he said he had better summon some troops from Finsbury Fields.

But before he could do so, a loud cry of "Fire!" came from Barbican Street; and when the location of this latest menace was learned, it was Sheriff Sheldon's own house! The sheriff left in a hurry with a crowd at his heels, Kip among them.

The new conflagration was a small one and was soon under control. Kip departed for home, weary, puzzled, uneasy. You might almost say he departed unnoticed.

One of Mr. Pepys' journal entries, made later, tells the outcome of this business, at least partially:

To the Sessions-house [the court at Old Bailey Prison] . . . *and so got up to the Bench, my Lord Chief-Justice Keeling being Judge. . . . Here were several fine trials; among others, several brought in for making it their trade to set houses on fire merely to get plunder; and all proved by two little boys* [the pushcart boys] . . . *who did give so good account of particulars that I never heard children in my life. And I confess, though I was unsatisfied with the force given to such little boys, to take away men's lives, yet, when I was told that my Lord Chief-Justice did declare that there was no law against taking the oath of children above twelve years old, and then heard from Sir R. Ford the good account which the boys had given of their understanding the nature and consequence of an oath, and now my own observation of the sobriety and readiness of their answers . . . I was fully satisfied that they ought to have as much credit as the rest. . . . And it is worth considering how unsafe it is to have children play up and down this lewd town.* [Two other youthful witnesses], *one my Lady Montagu's son, I know not what Lady Montagu's, and the other of good condition* [Mordant], *were playing in Moore-Fields* [a year or two before], *and one rogue, Gabriel Holmes, did come to them and teach them to drink, and then to bring him plate and clothes from their fathers' houses, and carry him into their houses, leaving open the doors for him, and at last were made of Holmes' conspiracy, and were at the very burning of this house in Aldersgate Street, on Easter Sunday last, and did gather up goods, as they had resolved before: and this Gabriel Holmes did advise to have had two houses set on fire, one after another, that, while they were quenching of one, they might be burning another. And it is pretty that G. Holmes did tell his fellows, and these boys swore it, that he did set fire to a box of linen in the Sheriffe, Sir Joseph Shelden's house, while he was attending the fire in Aldersgate Street, and the Sheriffe himself said that there was a fire in his house, in a box of linen, at the same time, but cannot conceive how this fellow could do it. The boys did swear against Gabriel Holmes that he made it his part to pull the plug out of the engine while it was a-playing; and it really was so. And goods they did carry away, and the manner of setting the house on fire was, that Holmes did get to a public cockpit and set fire to the straw in it with a fire-ball . . . and burned the house; and among other things they carried away, he took six of the cocks that were at the cockpit; and afterwards the boys told us how they had one dressed, but it was so hard they could not eat it. But that which was most remarkable was the impudence of this Holmes, who hath been arraigned often, and still got away; and on this business was taken, and broke loose just at Newgate Gate; and was last night luckily taken about Bow, where he got loose, and run into the river, and hid himself in the rushes; and they pursued him with a dog, and the dog got him and held him till he was taken. But the impudence of this fellow was such, that he denied he ever saw the boys before . . . but was found guilty of the act of burning the house, and other things that he stood indicted for.*

Here Mr. Pepys drops the matter. But *Smith's Obituary* tells us that Gabriel Holmes was hanged on July 11, 1667, and buried in the new churchyard in the fields in Cripplegate parish.

Let us hope his sad end would be forever a warning to Kobet, last heard from in Bridewell's workhouse; to Montagu and Mordant, who had been lured to crime through idleness and boredom; to the parents of Montagu and Mordant, who had been too lavish with money, too meager with love; to the pushcart boys, who dared to testify truly; to Little Parker, who had touched the fringe of crime without recognizing it.

As for Kip, when he realized that he had been used for thievery, shame engulfed him. Yet he was thankful that he had escaped arrest and was not called to testify. After all, he was not "of their conspiracy." As the weeks passed, he came to believe that he was in no way involved.

And, indeed, he would have been fortunately in the clear had not Shark happened upon him at Bedlam's fence that day. Shark saw him pass the coat and hat through the fence to Nath Sunday and was vastly interested. Afterward he followed Kip to Aldersgate Street and there, loitering and peering, he pieced out a pattern of delinquency for a future report.

Because of this, Kip must walk under a darkening cloud, vulnerable and unaware.

Mr. Pepys' diary entry for Saturday, May 12, ends thus:

This day came home again my girle Susan, her sicknesse proving an ague, and she had a fit as soon almost as she came home. The fleete is not yet gone from the Nore. The plague encreases in many places, and is 53 this week with us.

Susan was embarrassed to be taken with a chill while unpacking her clothes. It meant that she must climb into bed and cover herself warmly for a few hours. The new cook, a sedate little woman with gray hair, was a stranger to her, and this was rather frightening. What if she objected to sharing a room with a sick girl she'd never met?

But the woman was kind and reasonable. "You look to be still under the weather, girl," she said. "Take the bed that used to be yours. I'll put away your clothes. I'm Mrs. Mary Moore. When I was a girl, I had the ague, myself." She brought Susan some hot tea and told her not to exert herself. "When you get done shaking, you'll warm up and sweat, we both know that. You'll soon be on your feet, able to help me a little."

Susan kissed the ministering hand and wept.

"Now, now," the new cook scolded, "none of that! Think of yourself as lucky. Those that entertain the ague can hardly get the plague. They've built up a cute strength that others lack."

"I'm crying because my mother has just died," Susan explained.

"What?" Mary Moore was reasonably startled.

"She went to sleep last Sunday night and didn't wake up. She'd not been sick. I mean, not with a fever or any such thing. She faded away, Mrs. Moore. That's the nearest I can tell you."

"Had she been weak and pale a long while?"

"Yes, she had been. She denied herself enough to eat, so there'd be more for her two little boys and her husband—that's my stepfather, the sexton of St. Bride's. She'd been getting frailer all winter, and he hadn't noticed it."

"But she fetched you to Westminster around May Day, didn't she? Mrs. Pepys told me so."

"Yes, Mr. Pepys sent for her when I fell sick, and she made two trips here that day, to arrange to move me. It must have been hard for her, Mrs. Moore, but she never let on how tired she was."

"Now, now! Let's not talk. Your teeth's chattering."

But Susan could not refrain. "Her husband wouldn't let me in their house—not that I blame him, for it might have been a contagion I had. My mother knew it wasn't, though, and she found me a nurse and lodged me next door to her. Mr. Pepys paid the costs. It was good of him. We were grateful."

"Quit talking now," Mary Moore said kindly.

"You won't tell anybody about her dying? The Pepyses would think it was the plague, and I'd be sent away again."

"I won't open my mouth about it, Susan."

"I've not got any place to go, you see. The sexton's widowed sister has moved to his house. She'll take care of the little ones. She looks to be kind."

"You can be thankful for that. Drink the tea now."

"Yes. . . . And I've got something else to be thankful for, Mrs. Moore. My mother wasn't buried in the parish outfields, as so many are now. She's sleeping in a pretty corner of St.

Bride's Yard. The church yard was thought to be full, but the sexton had held back a little space, under some honeysuckle vines. Some day I can have a small stone put there, with her name and dates on it. Oh, I'm fortunate, Mrs. Moore!"

But though Susan turned her face to the wall and thought gratefully of this good fortune, her tears continued to flow for the sweet and gentle mother who was gone.

Susan measured up to Mrs. Moore's expectations and was able to do her share of the work in a few days' time.

The immediate past was like a dream, such being the effects of ague. Mingling with the vague mists of her recent fevers was the memory of her mother's death, like something that had happened long ago. It was as if she had grieved a long time; had worn proper mourning for a year; had laid floral wreaths for every season (in her feverish dreams she had done so, even holly at Christmas); and now had come, full circle, to late springtime again, though but a brief time had passed.

Mrs. Moore had some news for Susan, not yet divulged: a boy who seemed to be her sweetheart had come looking for her last Sunday and had said he would come again as soon as he could. Mrs. Moore delayed telling her for a reason. Her theory was, if the boy failed to appear Sunday afternoon, that being the courting time for young men who labored, Susan might go into a tizzy of disappointment. Anyway, let her get her strength back before exciting her. Had Mrs. Moore known of Susan's yearnings and anxieties, she would not have delayed.

At midweek, while Susan was shelling peas for dinner, Mrs. Mary Moore broke the news. "Your sweetheart came here looking for you, Sunday a-week-agone. He's been laid up with his eyes, he said, but now he's back at work at the Lime House kilns. They're all well, otherwise, he said."

"All well!" Susan repeated ringingly in awe and relief. It was as if she must sing it to the rafters. "For all I knew, something had happened to Amos. Or, anyway, to his family."

"When I told him you'd been taken home, sick, he was mighty upset. So I told him what I'd figured out; that you were just worn to a frazzle from hard work after cook Alice left."

"Oh, Mrs. Moore! I can't thank you enough for this news about Amos! How did he look?"

The kind woman hesitated, not permitting herself to say, "Like a scarecrow," which was on the tip of her tongue.

"Please, Mrs. Moore! Did Amos seem himself?"

"As I'd never laid eyes on your Amos previous to that day, Susan, I'm not fit to say. Has he always been rawboned?"

"When I first knew him, he wasn't." Susan's hands came to rest among the pods while she looked dreamily out of the window. "He was built just right."

"Hm-m-m. How about his eyes?"

"Blue," replied Susan reverently. "Sky blue."

"Never mind the color, dear. I mean, were they always weak?"

"Weak? Why, no, Mrs. Moore. His eyelids were red from firing, but that didn't weaken his eyes."

"They seem to be in a bad way now, Susan. I'd be at fault not to tell you. But he's on the mend, he said."

"Then he wants me not to worry, Mrs. Moore."

When Susan had finished shelling the peas she put them to cook with salted water and a chunk of butter, the way Mrs. Pepys relished them. Then she went to the open door and looked across at Navy Yard garden, which was well tended and smelled of bloom. The sunlight, the blooms, the health that had returned to her body, the knowledge that Amos still lived and was concerned for her—these things made her feel resurrected. Nothing seemed too hard to cope with now, not even the ague, though she knew it might strike again. She would win each bout, she would finally conquer it; and some day she would tell her children, "When I was a young girl, I used to have the ague."

This state of normalcy was everywhere that day. London would outlast the plague. The English Fleet, mismanaged and poorly victualed though it was, alerted itself downriver to meet the well-fed Dutch. Mr. and Mrs. Pepys had gone from home for the day but would surely return, Susan knew, late for supper, arguing, kissing, quarreling, talking of great things and small. In this confusion, Susan somehow felt secure.

On the Skeet houseboat too, this was a time of adjustment.

Kip had not mentioned his shady adventures in Aldersgate Street, but now he could no longer contain himself. When he and Amos were cooling themselves on the deck that evening, he made a quick confession. "You know I used to go, now and again, to Aldersgate Street, Amos. There were some boys over there that treated me fine, and I didn't know they were crooked. I didn't catch on till Easter Day, when those fires broke out."

Amos, startled, sat up straight and peered at Kip in the dusk. Everybody knew about that business because Sheriff Sheldon had made a stir about it. "*Were you in that mess, Kip?*"

"Yes, but I wasn't caught. I helped the gang move some stuff out o' the tavern, just to save it from burning. I mean, that's what I thought I was doing."

Amos jumped to his feet and began slapping Kip with the flat of his hand, getting in the licks wherever he could land them. It must also be said that he cursed his brother shockingly. "So it's looting you've been up to, you little fool!"

"Shut up!" Kip yelled. "Nobody can curse me and call me a looter! I told you I didn't know what I'd got into!" Enraged by the injustice of Amos's charges, he doubled his fists and lunged in retaliation. Amos, still shaky from his illness, fell sprawling to the deck, cutting his chin on a winch.

Singer tugged at his rope and barked fiercely; and Mrs. Skeet, who was cooking supper, came running with a spoon that dripped gravy. "What's amiss?" she cried. "What's took place?"

Amos got to his feet, watching Kip cautiously. "Nothin' to speak of. I let fly at Kip when I oughtn't had."

It was an apology, and Kip unclenched his fists. Both boys stood silent, breathing hard.

"What was it about?" Mrs. Skeet insisted. "Won't neither of ye tell a person why ye fought?"

"It's all over now," Amos said evasively, and to Kip's relief. Then he felt his swelling jaw, saw blood on his fingers, laughed. "You've got a good punch, Kip."

Kip was properly modest. "I couldn't a-knocked you down if you hadn't been wobbly on your feet."

Amos started to the boat's edge to wash his face, but Mrs. Skeet tugged at his elbow. "Don't wash your cut in the dirty Thames," she advised. "Come get a basin o' water from the conduit. Then ye can put arnica on, to keep down the swellin'."

Mrs. Skeet was puzzled by her offspring, as are all mothers at times, but she trusted in their decency. Kip had been up to something, that was certain, and Amos had corrected him. So be it. She had troubles enough already, what with Amos's recent illness, and his wages stopping for several weeks, and the plague taking off her friends. She was worried, too, about Susan Stokes. Amos had accepted the opinion of the new cook at the Pepys house, that Susan was more tired than ill. But she herself was apprehensive for Susan's health. And where in all London would Amos find another girl so fine and true?

Mrs. Skeet admired Susan and wanted her for Amos. She knew that marriage can take a man forward, or it can hold him back. She knew that she, Nan Skeet, had never taken her husband forward, or her sons either. Her addiction to drink had been a detriment to the family, like an undertow, tugging to pull them off course. That her boys were decent and ambitious was a wonder to her.

The Skeets sat down to supper with perfect amity, the boys showing no resentment toward each other. However Mrs. Skeet found them depressingly quiet, and she thought they ate from duty, rather than from appetite.

"Don't ye relish the stew?" she asked in disappointment.

"It's tasty," Amos assured her.

"It's prime," Kip said.

"Well, it's a rule I got from Mrs. Alice when we went to Navy Yard in October. It's called Sallymagundy—that's French for stew. Ye can make it with herring or beef or lamb, whichever ye've got."

"And we've got herring," Kip said grimly.

"Speakin' of Navy Yard, as I was," said Mrs. Skeet, "when are ye to go there again, Amos, to ask after Susan Stokes?"

"This Sunday coming," Amos answered.

"You don't have to remind 'im, Muv," Kip told her.

The boys left the supper table and went to the deck, letting their mother know, by their brusqueness, that they did not want her to follow.

"Kip," Amos said when they were alone, "start at the beginning and tell it straight." So Kip did, making a very good case for himself.

"You were easy taken in," Amos commented when he had finished. "You were easy used. As easy as Parker, the kid you say is just twelve years old."

"I was hoodwinked," Kip replied with dignity. This large, new word, properly applied and honestly used, served him as a shield, and he stood his ground behind it. "I was hoodwinked from start to finish."

"For a Montagu to be mixed up in a thing like that," Amos said, "that surprises me a good deal. I wonder if he's any kin to Lady Anne?"

"He's her cousin, all right. I asked him."

Amos fell to brooding. Kip wondered if he was thinking about his, Kip's, troubles, or about Anne Montagu, who used to make a fuss over him in the Pepys back yard. He wished he knew. If Amos was still mooning over that girl, then he'd relish saying to him, "It looks like there's more than one fool in the Skeet family!"

After a time Amos remarked that he was tired and would go to bed. "When six o'clock comes every morn," he said, "I can't hardly make myself get up."

"Well, good night," Kip answered. "I can't turn in, myself, till I've put dill in the fish tubs." He was surprised that Amos gave him no advice or warnings about his future conduct. But, then, Amos was never one to waste words. He had named the gang's crimes, and his hand had struck hard; that, after all, was a plenty.

Susan repaired her clothes that week. She had grown taller in the past year, and hems must be let out. She also mended a dress that Mercer had given her, planning to wear it for Amos.

But even though engrossed with herself, Susan noticed that Mary Moore, the cook, had begun to limp. She remarked on it when they were preparing a "company dinner" for the five Houblon brothers, those wealthy seagoing merchants whom Mr. Pepys cultivated.

"Sit down and rest, Mrs. Moore," she urged. "I'll watch the stove and brown the veal."

"That's good of you, child. Just a half-hour off my feet would help."

While she rested, Mary Moore confessed to Susan that she was not so strong as she pretended to be. "I'll be fifty years old this autumn, and my ankles swell. I doubt if I'll be able to hold out here."

"They like your meals, Mrs. Moore, and the way you serve them up. Mrs. Pepys said she can tell you're used to cooking for gentry."

Mrs. Moore laughed shortly. "I was used to leisure when I was young, Susan. My father was a squire. My born name would surprise the Pepyses. But fortunes change. My father's horses were shod by a smithy named John Clarges. Clarges' daughter is now the Duchess of Albemarle, having married General Monck. But maybe that's the way the world should be, Susan, a seesaw—some going up and up while others come down." She got to her feet and made a tasty sauce for the asparagus while Susan watched, to learn.

"I'll help you all I can, Mrs. Moore," Susan promised. "I'll always get the breakfasts, because I'm used to it. I do want you to hold out here."

"Thank you, child. It's a trying house to serve."

"One of the hardest in London," Susan admitted. "At least I've heard other servants say so. You never know what to expect, no matter if you're a cook or a chambermaid or a page, or even a companion like Mercer, for nothing's planned. But I'll tell you something, Mrs. Moore, it's hardly ever dull here."

Especially was it not dull for Susan the following day, a Friday. Mr. Pepys arose at five and called her awake to get his breakfast. This she was able to do by the time he had shaved and dressed. While he was drinking his small beer he mentioned that he would bring home some lobsters to be cooked for dinner. "Have the big pot boiling by two o'clock," he instructed.

"Yes, Mr. Pepys. Will the lobsters be dead or squirming? If they're still alive, Mrs. Moore will have to drop them in."

"They'll be alive. I'm not fetching them from Deptford, only from Nokes' market."

"Nokes' market?" Susan repeated in surprise. "Do you mean that fish dock at Dick's Shore?"

"Yes, that's the place. It's close to old Lime House. I'll stop there as I come upriver. Nokes has the best lobsters hereabout, I've heard, and I want to try them."

"Mr. Pepys," Susan said with quick entreaty, "I'll ask a favor. While you're at Nokes' place, notice the houseboat tied at his wharf. It's the home of the Skeet family. The Skeet boys used to bring those pickled herring you liked so much. They had to stop coming to Navy Yard because they don't belong to the Fishmongers' Company."

"All right, I'll notice the shanty boat, Susan. Hurry on with my bacon, please."

"Yes, sir." She hurried and soon set the dish before him, a sizzling rasher, garnished with chicken livers. "But, Mr. Pepys," she said, hovering, "I want you to do more than notice. I'd be grateful if you'd hollo the houseboat and talk to somebody

—just anyone who answers. Ask how Amos Skeet is feeling. Ask when he'll be able to come to see Susan Stokes again."

"Odd zooks!" Pepys exclaimed. "Is there disease at that dock? Is somebody sick there?"

"No, Mr. Pepys, not the way you're thinking! Amos Skeet's eyes have been affected by fire and smoke, that's all. He works at Lime House kilns, making quicklime. He was laid up for several weeks. After he could get about, he came here to see me. But it was when I was away, and I missed him."

Pepys looked at Susan sharply. "So you've got a sweetheart." He did not seem pleased. He forever dreaded to lose a good servant, and Susan was their greatest bargain. She was still an apprentice. When he confided to his journal the wages paid out to his servants he did not have to include Susan's, for she received none.

"I do have a sweetheart, Mr. Pepys," Susan replied bravely. "We're not pledged to one another, but I hope for that. I keep hoping with all my might. It's this way; I know I love him dearly, but he doesn't know if he loves me."

"You're young, Susan, and you can do better than a lime burner. I advise you to tarry. Don't push this romance." He finished his well-cooked breakfast and remarked as he got up to go, "I'm going to pay you regular wages from now on. You can count on it. Two pounds a year, in addition to gifts."

"Oh, Mr. Pepys! Thank you!" But her pleasure was tempered with disappointment, for he had not promised to carry her message.

Before noon Samuel Pepys stopped briefly at his house and left a net of lobsters at the scullery door. "They're freshly killed," he told Susan, "so you won't have to cope with their claws. Have dinner at three. And, by the way, Susan," he said over his shoulder, "there's a very fine sea shell in that net for you! I picked it up this morning at Blackwall."

Susan called her thanks to him, but without effusion. The favors she had received from Mr. Pepys this day could not make up for the fact that he had brought her no message from the Skeets, though he had been close enough to speak the boat without straining his voice.

To help eat the lobster for dinner came one Mr. Holyard, Pepys' surgeon. The man seemed to have an uncanny way of knowing when the Pepyses were having special dishes for dinner, such as lobster or pheasant, and he would put in an appearance as they sat down at table.

Susan, seeing him today just as she was ready to carry in the dinner, alerted the cook. "Mrs. Moore, Mr. Holyard's come to dinner—that man I told you about! I'll leave the door ajar, so you can listen."

"Yes, do!" Mary Moore answered. "I'd enjoy to hear him go on."

Mr. Holyard (of a mysterious origin) sometimes told of his adventures in far countries, now and then lapsing into Latin, so Mrs. Pepys and the servants could not follow him. At other times he ranted against persons in high places whom he disliked; the London physicians especially, because they excluded surgeons from their fellowship. Holyard had operated on Samuel Pepys for a kidney stone several years before. Indeed, he had successfully cut more people for that ailment than any surgeon in London. At St. Thomas's Hospital for the poor and lame of Southwark, he gave his talents blithely, both for amputations and the stone. At bloodletting too, he excelled. When bleeding Mr. Pepys, he would draw sixteen ounces at a time, compliment his rich blood, and charge him five shillings. "Lie on your back a while," he would say, "then you can walk to Westminster, as good as new." Lately he had been trying to catch Tom Edwards; for Tom often complained of stomach ache, and Mr. Pepys thought his page should either be bled or cut of the stone at the hands of an expert. So far, Tom had been able to avoid these ministrations with the help of Susan. When Mr. Holyard came to the house she would warn him, and he would take off to another part of town.

Today there was no time to warn Tom. However Mr. Holyard was in a quiet mood, enjoying the lobster and talking reasonably, not even lambasting the London physicians. His medical theories were mild: he advised Mr. Pepys to eat gruel for breakfast, and to partake freely of roasted apples, rye bread, and butter.

Susan apologized for him in the kitchen. "I don't know what's the matter with Mr. Holyard today. He's not himself. He's not demented."

Next day there came to dinner another person intriguing to Susan, and she invited Mrs. Moore to apply her eye to the crack in the door. The guest was Anthony Deane, the young shipwright who had taught Mr. Pepys mathematics and timber measurement.

"He's the one who gave Mr. Pepys that darling ship model," she whispered with a sigh. She wanted the toy ship so intensely that she sometimes prayed God to forgive her for coveting it. She wanted to give it to Amos Skeet, because Amos craved a ship model and had tried to build one, failing out of sheer awkwardness.

Susan and Mrs. Moore were not disappointed in the table talk.

Mr. Pepys ordered up a bottle of wine from the cellar, and he and Mrs. Pepys toasted the *Rupert*, the ship Mr. Deane had built for the Navy at Harwich, calling it "the best ship that ever was built." Mr. Deane was not modest. He praised his own skill; he declared he was a greater designer than Christopher Pett. "I'm the first man to figure a ship's draft before she's launched!" he exulted. Then he told of his new cannon, the little Punchinello, that would transform the English Navy.

Unlike Mr. Holyard of the day before, Mr. Deane hardly noticed the food. "Won't you have more of the new peas, sir?" Susan urged. . . . "Won't you try the stewed Morocco plums, sir?"

She longed to ask, each time she presented a dish at his elbow, "Can't you spare me just one little ship, sir, for Amos?" And so her voice was so imploring that Mrs. Pepys wondered at it, and tugged at her skirt and whispered, "Don't nag a guest to eat, Susan! Let the man be!"

Thus had passed the week for Susan. A time of muted sorrow, accepted. A return to life and curiosity, and to the hopeful dreams of love.

When Sunday came Susan was quite keyed up. She broke a crock and spilled a jug of vinegar. "I'm jumpy because I'm uncertain," she said, mopping up. "I'm wondering if Amos will come today."

"I wouldn't be surprised if he comes, Susan," Mary Moore said. "Help me with dinner, then give no thought to supper. It's a sunny day for walking, in case he comes and asks you."

"In case he comes and asks me," Susan repeated breathlessly, and dropped the bread knife.

"That's the sign a man's coming," Mrs. Moore reminded her. "Come now, get control of your hands and your wits. Help me to put these capons to bake."

During the morning the house grew quiet. Mr. and Mrs. Pepys left for Morning Prayer at St. Olave's. Mercer departed for dinner at her own home nearby, taking Will Hewer with her; for Mr. Hewer was about to rent lodgings in the Mercer house, to get away from Samuel Pepys' perpetual domination. (Pepys even told him how to wear his cape, and sometimes he slapped him.) Jane Gentleman and Tom Edwards, both, had been granted a day's leave. They went off together with a lunch basket and Tom's guitar—Susan enviously watching—bound for Spring Garden.

"Will the Pepyses bring company home for dinner?" Susan wondered, not knowing how to set the table.

"None's been spoken of, so set places for two. Mrs. Pepys told me to cook the fowl and make fritters; that was all she asked for. But I'm adding a salad of endive and beets."

Lord's Day. With my wife to church. [Wrote Mr. Pepys of that morning.] *At noon dined mighty nobly, ourselves alone.*

Susan, serving them, thought they seemed remarkably contented. She walked softly and spoke as little as possible, so as not to disturb them.

"Mrs. Moore," she reported in the kitchen, "they're holding hands across the table! They're recalling a Sunday when they were first married and had only bread and pickled pork for dinner."

"Glory be," Mrs. Moore replied. "Mayhap they'll spend this day together without friend or foe to come between."

"No, they're going their separate ways this afternoon," Susan said regretfully. "Mr. Pepys has to go to Westminster. Mrs. Pepys and Mercer are going to Greenwich in a hackney coach."

"Whatever for, I wonder."

"Mrs. Pepys is going to be a gossip," Susan stated sadly. "It's dreadful, but I heard them say so. She'll gossip with the Daniels."

Mrs. Moore laughed. "That means she'll be a godparent, Susan. A body can tell you were born and raised in London, not to know that. Mr. Pepys' family came from Cambridgeshire, like mine, so we use some of the same old words. Gossip comes from the words God and sib—that's a blood relative. Mrs. Pepys is going to hold the Daniel baby at the font and be his godsib, or gossip."

"Oh, dear," Susan said, relieved. "I've only known the other meaning of gossip, the kind my mother warned me against."

After the Pepyses had departed and the last cooking vessel had been scoured, Mary Moore and Susan retired to the room near the kitchen, which they shared. Mrs. Moore took off her shoes and began to read a book of homilies, nodding a little. Susan bathed and put on the dress she had altered.

Mrs. Moore glanced up. "My, you're pretty!" she said in surprise.

Susan's hair curled willfully from the kitchen dampness. Her skin was normal again, freed of pallor. On her left cheek she wore a tiny heart-shaped black patch; on her left arm, a black ribbon. Mrs. Moore studied her anxiously. "If your lad fails to come, Susan, don't give way to melancholy. Don't do anything rash, like walking the Bridge by yourself."

"I promise, Mrs. Moore. They say a patch means 'come and get me,' so I've put on the mourning band to balance me."

"What's that sweet smell, Susan?"

"It's a lotion Mrs. Pepys gave me, spiced with clove pinks. I hope you'll get a good nap, Mrs. Moore. Here's a footstool."

Susan went and sat on the front steps. And there, half an hour later, she witnessed two ill-sorted arrivals. She sat as if frozen. Along Hart Street came the big coach-and-four of Lord Montagu, complete with footman. Out of Seething Lane, bending to the incline, came Amos Skeet, trudging.

The Montagu coachman reined in smartly at the Pepys house, and the footman leaped from his perch and opened the coach door, revealing three female figures: Lady Paulina Montagu, Lady Anne Montagu, and their chaperon, the old French governess.

Lady Anne stepped to the cobblestones. Amos stopped short a few paces from her, straightened his back, stared. Lady Anne returned his look at her leisure. "Are you Amos Skeet?" she asked him gropingly.

"Yes, Lady Anne."

"But you can't be!" She smiled, frowned, and shrugged, all at once. "I mean, aren't you different?"

He felt his features, ran his hand through his hair. "I do be Amos Skeet," he insisted quaintly. Susan thought his phrasing was like his mother's, and so was the accent. It was as if he had carried those tones within him always, and had never used them until this moment.

Anne turned toward the coach, said to the chaperon and to Lady Paulina: "Mamselle and Paulina, this is Mr. Skeet, a friend of Susan Stokes, the maid."

"How d'j'do," the two ladies said in languid concert.

"And the same to both of you," replied Amos stiffly. He stepped aside and stood against the hedge.

Without glancing at him again, Lady Anne walked toward

the Pepys house. Susan got up from the steps and went to meet her. "Good evening, Lady Anne," Susan said, though it was not evening.

"How d'j'do, Susan. You're expecting company, I see. Is my Cousin Samuel Pepys at home?"

"No, Lady Anne. Mr. Pepys has gone to Westminster. And Mrs. Pepys has gone to Greenwich to be a godmother."

"That's too bad," said Lady Anne, looking put out. "We wanted Cousin Sam to take us down to the ships. Father's gone as Ambassador to Spain, you know, and we've got nobody to take us to the ships. We're asked for tea on the *Ruby*—"

"No, Anne," came Paulina's petulant voice from the coach, "on the *Rainbow*."

"Oh, well, the one or the other. We're dying to go. It's so gay at the ships just before they sail. Lieutenant Carteret—he's our brother-in-law's cousin—has bid us come. His ship's still at Lea Roads. Mother says we can spend the night ashore there, if Mamselle approves. But of course," she concluded, "Mother expected Cousin Sam to advise us."

"Come, Anne!" Paulina called. "We'll go on without him!"

"Oh, do, let's!" Anne answered jubilantly, and ran back to the coach and entered it. She remembered to wave to Susan as they departed, but she had already forgotten Amos. He stood crowded against the hedge, looking after the great coach in a strange way. Susan went noiselessly into the house and closed the door, not willing to be a witness to his hurt pride.

She waited tensely. Suppose Amos should go straightway home and not come back? He might want to wipe out the very memory of Navy Yard, because it was here, and here only, that he had known Anne Montagu. Was it taking too great a risk, to leave him standing there alone? Perhaps, but she forced herself to wait.

In a little while, not nearly so long as it seemed to Susan, the heavy knocker creaked and pounded. She opened the door, and there stood Amos. He was rawboned, he was red-eyed, and his face was swollen one-sidedly from his fight with Kip. He had temporarily lost all his good looks except his well-knit body.

"Well, Susan—" he said uncertainly.

She threw her arms around him and drew down his face and pressed her cheek to his. "My darling, darling," she murmured, "I've not seen you for weeks! I've worried so!"

"You have, Susan?" His surprise was the greater because of the humiliation he had just suffered. A moment ago he had seen himself reflected in Lady Anne's eyes as plain, unimportant, undesirable. When she had exclaimed that he couldn't be Amos Skeet, she had meant, "How could I have fondled your homely face?" and her wonder was tinged with amusement. She was ridiculing her own former taste. Then she had closed the matter by forgetting that he stood there, hat in hand, waiting to bid her good-by.

Amos straightened, needing to look at Susan, wondering if she were pitying him. What he saw in her face was not pity, but he could not cope with it; his new shyness stood in the way. "Susan," he asked in perplexity, "why are you wearing a beauty patch and a black band?"

"The patch is because I've grown up, Amos. The mourning band is for my mother."

"Your mother! I didn't know, Susan, or I'd have been quicker to come here."

She told him what had happened, holding back the tears.

"She was pushed past her strength," Amos said. "I expect you'll miss her a good deal. A sweet lady, we thought, Kip and me."

"You've no idea how good and gentle she was," Susan said.

"I hoped to know her better," Amos said stiffly, honestly.

Susan began to weep quietly. She was turning away when Amos took hold of her and drew her to him. "I love you, girl," he said in surprise. He kissed the top of her head. Then he kissed her face and awkwardly found his way to her lips.

When Susan finally turned her face away, he spoke what needed to be said. "I've spent my hoardings because I was laid off from work," he told her. "But when I've saved something again, will you pledge to marry me, Susan?"

"I pledge now, Amos. And I'll wait for you, however long."

"You're the kindest girl in the world, Susan, and the truest and sweetest. Your skin smells like gillyflowers." Hearing himself say such things, Amos was astonished and confused. He had heard idle young men going up and down the river in barges and yawls, reciting to a lute about love. Sometimes, by starlight, such sentiments were very affecting, drifting over the water to where he sat on the houseboat. But here in the Pepys hall, coming from himself, a limey, it must be laughable.

Susan, though, did not laugh. She was thrilled and comforted. She thought humbly that she must not let him know how much she loved him. For all men were alike, she'd heard said, in one way: they would never value fruit that fell too easily. "Always keep the upper hand," cook Alice used to say with a wink while knitting stockings and dispensing advice in those long winter evenings of the plague. And she could tell many a sad story, to illustrate. Usually she concluded with her favorite adage: "A maid touched lightly while unwed, is sooner to the altar led."

Susan was now confronted with the servant-maid's greatest problem—where to take her young man.

"I don't think Mr. Pepys would want you in here," she told Amos regretfully. "He went to Westminster, but he might come home at any time, and company with him."

"Could we sit in the kitchen, then?" Amos asked.

"No, Amos, I won't, I won't sit in the kitchen today! I've been in it since early morning. Besides, I've got on a new dress, don't you notice?"

"So you have," he admitted. "Leastwise, I never saw it before."

"There's a place to sit not far away," Susan said, "if you don't mind a lot of other couples around you."

She took him to "the ruins," as Mr. Pepys called the area, just off Seething Lane. It was what remained of the Priory of Crutched Friars, destroyed long ago, at the time of the Dissolution. Henry VIII had turned the floor of the great church into a tennis court, and had permitted glass blowers to set up shop in the refectory hall. Columns, arches, half-fallen walls covered with ivy stood here and there. Slabs of stone lay amid the ruins, like austere benches. As on any fine Sunday, a score of lovers sat about today, holding hands and telling their love; finding the only innocent privacy available to them in crowded east London. Perhaps of all the Tudor's desecrations, none had turned out so happily as this one.

Susan and Amos found a niche that suited them, and soon Amos's strong callused hands were holding Susan's small callused hands, stroking and caressing them. They tried to inform each other of what had happened. Susan told how her mother's death was like a dream to her, because of her own illness. She said her mother's few possessions were all claimed by the sexton. "So I've not got *even a quilt* for my dowry, Amos! But Mr. Pepys is going to pay me two pounds sterling for this coming year's service, and that will buy our bedding."

Amos told of Kip's experiences in Aldersgate Street.

Susan was horrified. "I remember I encouraged him to go there," she confessed. "I thought he was earning honest money."

"So did my mother. So did Kip, for that matter. But Kip's never chary about walking into danger. I'll have to keep closer watch on him from now on."

"Has everything blown over about the looting, Amos?"

"Kip thinks so, but I'm not too sure. It could be we've not heard the last of that business."

"Why don't you go to the Parker boy's father, Amos? You could find him, knowing where he lives. Tell him your brother was as innocent of those Easter Day fires as his son was. Ask him what to do about it."

Amos considered. "No," he decided, "I won't ask a stranger's help. Anyway, there's no use calling Kip to his attention. It just might give the man some hold over Kip."

"It's wonderful, how you think things out," Susan marveled.

"I can take care of my own brother, I expect," Amos told her. In her face there was admiration and trust; he basked in the light of them, sure of his strength.

The summer was the happiest Susan had ever known. It had no right to be, for the plague held on, though abating; and the war with Holland persisted; and Mrs. Mary Moore quit the kitchen and was replaced by a woman named Luce who was addicted to drinking and falling down stairs. The Pepyses quarreled more than ever, Mrs. Pepys scheming for new clothes and hair-styling, Mr. Pepys thwarting her. With himself, he was generous, refurbishing his study—his closet, he called it—until it was "one of the noblest in London." He ordered handsome presses for his books, purple serge draperies for his windows, maps for his walls, globes for his tables. He bought a "long glass," to study the stars from his leads. At his invitation friends came nightly to view the rings of Saturn and the mysteries of the moon through his telescope.

Through all the confusion, Susan moved serene. It was enough that she was loved by her beloved and they were often together. She proudly told Mr. and Mrs. Pepys that she was engaged to be married, and they treated her, she thought, with a new respect.

Mrs. Skeet, in a very ecstasy of satisfaction, invited her on Sundays to the houseboat. Kip would come and fetch her at midafternoon. After supper Amos would take her home through the dark ways of Whitechapel and Hart Street, to Seething Lane. Those occasions, touched with peril and poverty though they were, shone with gaiety for all of them.

Mrs. Skeet acknowledged the young couple's engagement with all the publicity she could summon, never losing a chance to speak of Susan as "Miss Stokes, my son's intended," an expression she considered elegant and adequate.

Another houseboat was alongside the wharf now, occupied by a decent couple named Tim and Sally Hooker, the man being Mr. Nokes' new employee. Though they seemed to be appalled by Mrs. Skeet in some ways, they were not unfriendly to her, not unneighborly. One day when a squall arose and both boys were absent from home, Mr. Hooker rescued Mrs. Skeet's laden clothesline before it blew away. Another time, he drove off a prowler for her.

The arrival of those neighbors solved a touchy problem for Amos: he and Susan need not live at the wharf when they were married, for Mrs. Skeet and Kip would have people within call, day and night. "I've decided we can take lodgings in Stepney next year," he told Susan, "just you and me! Two rooms on a ground floor will do us, won't it?"

Susan said it would do; indeed, it would do! She had not been able to picture life at the docks, even if they could have a shanty of their own. The great river was too menacing, the smells too heady, and sometimes Mr. Nokes' lobsters and turtles got loose and came visiting. Still and all, she would have consented to live there if Amos had asked it of her.

"I've never seen Stepney," she said, "but I'm sure it's heavenly nice. If we can't get lodgings on a ground floor, Amos, an upper floor will do, surely?"

"I've never lived up a stairs," Amos said doubtfully. "But I expect we'll have to take what's cheapest, to get a start." He said other things too, but they were spoken softly and meant for Susan alone, certainly not for Kip, who was eavesdropping.

Kip was not interested in their love-making, in fact it bored him, but he was always hoping to pick up a piece of news about himself. He had heard that Gabriel Holmes and Kobet had been caught and were to be tried. Would Amos attend the trials? Or was he planning to avoid them? Kip hesitated to ask, fearing it would roil Amos to talk about the wretched muddle.

Old Bailey trials were not announced in advance, and the Aldersgate cases were decided before Amos knew they were coming up. But he heard the talk, afterward. The penny news-sheets carried the story—much as Mr. Pepys recorded it in his diary—and Amos bought a paper in a tobacco shop. He took it to his Scots friend at the Lime House.

"I'd thank you to read me this newssheet, Mr. McTarvish," he requested. "Skip the war news and all. Just read me those trials that ran two days at Old Bailey, the man and boys that were caught setting fires and looting, Easter Day."

McTarvish found the piece and read it with a good deal of Scottish indignation. "Aye, that man's a scoundrel!" he stormed. "I can picture him now: mannerly, and dressed to the nines, but bitter ugly in his heart. Justice Keeling called him a corrupter of youth. Do you know any of these lads?"

"I don't know them," Amos replied cautiously, "but I've heard of them." He retrieved the paper from McTarvish's desk when he quit work, and carried it home. Susan would want to read it. She would be beside herself with joy to learn that Kip was not named at the trials.

It now seemed to Amos that Kip's cheerful outlook had been the sensible one, all along. He was not being sought. He had made a clean escape. That night he grudgingly admitted as much to Kip.

"McTarvish read me the trials out of this newssheet," he said, "and I listened for your name, but it ne'er came up. Little Parker's didn't, either. Montagu and Mordant testified, and so did the pushcart boys. They informed on Kobet—that boaster you told me about—and on Gabriel Holmes. They made things hot for the last one."

"We needn't ever tell Muv anything about that mess, Amos?"

"No, I reckon not. It would just stir her up. Besides, she couldn't hold her tongue. She'd tell the whole dock how you got taken in."

"But Susan knows, I'll bet. You tell that girl everything."

"Just about everything," Amos admitted. He could not understand the resentment in Kip's face. The resentment of a brother who thought himself supplanted.

Two months passed without worry or mishap, and September came in, as dry and brittle as a locust skin. Amos had found his lost good looks and was eagerly eyed by the girls when he went to Wapping for his tobacco. Susan was making chemises and nightgowns, having been given some linen yardage and blue ribbon by Mrs. Pepys. Kip was being taught to read by Mr. McTarvish, and making rapid strides, to his tutor's amazement. And Mrs. Skeet had done nothing outlandish in a long time.

Then the event that broke this lovely calm: London burned. Mr. Pepys tells it best.

September 2nd. Lord's-day. Some of our mayds sitting up late last night to get things ready against our feast today, Jane called us up about three in the morning, to tell us of a great fire they saw in the City. So I rose and slipped on my night-gowne and went to her window, and thought it to be on the back-side of Mark Lane at the farthest; but being unused to such fires as followed, I thought it far enough off; and so went back to bed again and to sleep. . . . By and by Jane comes and tells me that she hears that above 300 houses have been burned down tonight by the fire we saw, and that it is now burning down all Fish Street, by London Bridge. So I made myself ready presently, and walked to the Tower, and there got up upon one of the high places, Sir J. Robinson's little son going up with me; and there I did see the houses at that end of the Bridge all on fire, and an infinite great fire on this and the other side of the Bridge. . . . So I down to the water-side, and there got a boat and through bridge, and there saw a lamentable fire. . . . Everybody endeavouring to remove their goods, and flinging it into the river or bringing it to lighters that lay off; poor people staying in their houses till the very fire touched them, and then running into boats, or clambering from one pair of stairs by the water-side to another. Among

other things, the poor pigeons, I perceive, were loth to leave
their houses, but hovered about the windows and balconys till
they, some of them, burned their wings and fell down. . . .
The wind mighty high and driving it into the City; and every-
thing, after so long a drought, proving combustible, even the
very stones of churches.

A plan occurred to Mr. Pepys. He took boat to Whitehall,
the palace, and asked for an audience with the King and his
brother, the Duke of York.

Receiving him at once, they listened to his advice—*that un-*
less his Majesty did command houses to be pulled down, noth-
ing could stop the fire. They agreed to the necessity, but declined to take the responsibility. It was a royal Stuart custom
to let the Lord Mayor do the unpleasant work, and so the
King sent Pepys to tell that gentleman to proceed; they would
pledge him soldiers and laborers from the royal yards, they
said, to do his bidding. Pepys went without delay, *and there*
walked along Watling Street, as well as I could, every creature
coming away loaden with goods to save, and here and there
sick people, carried away in beds. At last met my Lord Mayor
in Canning Street, like a man spent, and delivered the King's
message.

Thus was inaugurated Pepys' plan for saving the City. And
so it happened that Amos Skeet became involved. For he was
presently one of the able-bodied young men who volunteered
to help the militia remove rubble from the path of the fire and
set off gunpowder to create gaps.

Having got things under way, Pepys remembered his dinner
party and went home to the scheduled "feast." Susan and Luce
had been hard at it all morning, never stopping to go to the
fire, though operating in a state of excitement. The dinner
was in honor of Miss Barbara Sheldon and young Mr. Wood,
the mastmaker's son. The Sheldons had sheltered Mrs. Pepys
and her two top maids in their Woolwich home during the
plague; but it was not so much gratitude that prompted this
party as it was snobbishness: Miss Sheldon had captured a

very rich young man; he was in partnership with his father, who imported masts from New England and sold them to the Navy. Barbara could now wear silk and jewels and move in high circles. Mr. Pepys was amazed that this could happen to a homely girl whose parents kept lodgers. He bluntly wrote of it: *A strange fortune for so odd a looked mayde, though her hands and body be good, and her nature very good, I think.*

We notice Miss Sheldon today because this good nature of hers, this kindness of heart, will serve Susan and Amos in their worst dilemma, before a year has passed.

When Susan announced dinner the guest of honor ran and kissed her, and nobody was surprised, for Barbara had shared her room with Susan a few days during the plague, and they were congenial. Susan whispered in Barbara's ear, "I'm going to be married, too! I'm betrothed to Amos, the boy I told you about."

Barbara exclaimed in delight, and they would have talked together more, but Mrs. Pepys drew Barbara away because Mr. Pepys was about to offer a toast, using their new goblets. Every one drank it, while young Mr. Wood stood with his arm around his bride's waist, and the smoke from burning London came in at the windows.

Wrote Pepys: *We had an extraordinary good dinner, and were as merry as at this time we could be.*

Dinner over, master, mistress, and guests left for the fire. Soon the upper servants followed, and only Susan and Luce remained. It was at the big pewter dishwashing basin that Amos found Susan, toward dusk.

"I've washed myself at old man Batten's water spigot," he told her, and kissed her ardently, pushing the curls back from her forehead because she could not do it for herself. "I've not got time to stay," he said, and told her about his activities.

"Do let somebody else light the gunpowder," Susan begged.

"Look here, Susan, I'm not in his Majesty's Navy, but that don't mean I'm afraid to set off a charge. Have you seen Kip?"

When Susan said she had not, Amos was disappointed.

"I've got a feeling he's going to stay out all night," he said. "I wish I could find him and send him home." He left, frowning in anxiety, forgetting to kiss her good-by.

That evening the fire burned more fiercely, and Mr. Pepys wrote of it with an awful accuracy:

The wind great. As near the fire as we could, for smoke; and all over the Thames, with one's face in the wind, you were almost burned with a shower of fire-drops. . . . When we could endure no more upon the water, we to a little ale-house on the Bankside, over against the Three Cranes, and there staid till it was dark almost, and saw the fire grow. It appeared in corners and upon steeples, and between churches and houses, as far as we could see up the hill of the City, in a most horrid malicious bloody flame, not like the fine flame of an ordinary fire. Barbary and her husband away before us. We staid till, it being darkish, we saw the fire as one entire arch from this to the other side of the bridge, and in a bow up the hill for an arch a mile long: it made me weep to see it. The churches, houses, and all flaming at once; and a horrid noise the flames made, and the cracking of houses at their ruine. So home with a sad heart. . . . And the news coming every moment of the growth of the fire, we were forced to begin to pack our goods, and prepare for their removal; and did by moonshine, it being brave dry weather, carry much of my goods into the garden, and Mr. Hater and I did remove my money and iron chests into my cellar, as thinking that the safest place. . . . About four o'clock in the morning, my Lady Batten sent me a cart to carry away all my money and plate and best things to Sir W. Rider's at Bednall Green. Which I did, riding myself in my night-gowne in the cart. . . . Then home, with much ado to find a way, nor any sleep all that night to me nor my poor wife. But then, and all this day, she and I, and all my people labouring to get away the rest of our things . . . and we did carry them over Tower Hill . . . and down to a lighter which lay at the next quay, above the Tower Docke.

Susan's possessions were tied up in a sheet, but she refused to let Mr. Pepys take them away. She could not bear to think of her bridal underwear being tossed into a cart or a boat.

"If I must run for it," she told Mr. Pepys, "I'll carry my things with me. The bundle's not too heavy."

"Have it your own way, Susan," Pepys said. He was busily stripping the house of what movable objects yet remained—bedding, draperies, pictures, and clothing, to be added to the freight already consigned to the lighter on the river. His official papers had gone into a pit in Sir William Batten's back yard. His wines and Parmesan cheese had been lowered into Admiral Penn's excavation. In his excitement, Pepys laid several handsome books atop the cheese, and it is possible they wear the fragrance to this day.

It was Tuesday, and the fire was spreading to London's proudest fortress. To save it, houses were being razed in Tower Street.

Susan was almost out of her wits, what with loss of sleep, and trying to make do with the meals, and worrying about Amos, whom she had not seen since Sunday evening. When the explosions came, right on Tower Hill, she felt compelled to run and look for Amos there in the din. But it was no use. She was driven back by smoke and dust and falling stone, and by a great commotion of blasphemous men, none of whom was Amos Skeet. Returning distractedly to Navy Yard, she found herself worrying about Kip also. Had Amos ever located him, she wondered, or was he still roaming the City?

That day saw the burning of St. Paul's Cathedral, and the ruin of Cheapside. The Old Bailey was gutted, and Newgate Prison was made untenable. Along Fleet Street, the flames crept to the very walls of Inner Temple. Will Hewer removed his mother to Islington, her house in Pye Corner having burned; and Mr. Pepys could not send a letter to his father in the country because the Post-house was in ashes. Small new fires sprang up, unexplainably.

The Pepys household went to bed, but when they were

wakened by cries of fire in lower Seething Lane, Mrs. Pepys said she had had enough, and so did Jane Gentleman. Mr. Pepys put them aboard a boat owned by a friend named Proundy, and sent them to the Sheldons at Woolwich. With them went Mr. Pepys' gold—he had not taken it to Bednall Green with his silver—and Will Hewer to guard it. Mercer's safety did not have to be considered, for she had quit her job and returned home.

Susan might have gone to Woolwich, too; but she chose to remain at Navy Yard, with muddled old Luce for company. It was there that Amos would come seeking her, when he had a chance. If a girl is waiting for her lover, she is not afraid.

On Wednesday evening, Kip returned to Dick's Shore and came aboard the houseboat to Singer's glad barks. He had been absent from home since Sunday morning.

Mrs. Skeet received him joyfully. In her relief, she forgot the tongue-lashing she had stored up for him. He was disheveled, smoky, tattered, thin. He resembled an emaciated chimney sweep. In his pockets were nineteen shillings and twelvepence that he had earned, moving goods.

"I didn't o'ercharge anybody," he explained, laying his money on the table, "and some I didn't charge at all, the real poor ones with shabby stuff. Where's Amos?" he asked, freeing himself from his mother's embrace and patting Singer.

"He's searchin' for ye, Kip! He's not altogether doin' that, for he's a fire fighter, but he keeps on the lookout for ye, where'er he goes. I expect he'll beat ye, when he gets home."

"I expect he won't!" Kip said with spirit. He had just spent the most fabulous four days in his life, a willing worker in a great disaster, and what he had lost in pounds he had gained in maturity. Snatching sleep in doorways with other boys, buying buns and cheese when his stomach gnawed, he had fared very well, even though he had breathed too much smoke and had carried goods beyond his strength.

At Mrs. Skeet's urging, he washed himself while she cooked

him some bacon over charcoal. He wolfed it with bread and a mug of milk, and almost immediately tumbled into his bunk and slept. Dimly, he heard Amos come home; dimly heard the relief in Amos's voice on learning that he had returned; dimly heard Amos say, "I oughta beat the daylights out o' him, that's what." Then the smell of more bacon being broiled, and the sound of bread being sliced, as Mrs. Skeet happily fed her eldest.

Kip was deep in slumber when Amos picked up a sooty little bag from the floor and yanked it open. He poured some yellow coins onto the table, and the candlelight touched them prettily.

"What are they, Amos?" Mrs. Skeet asked, for she had never before seen a gold coin.

"They're guineas," Amos said. "Every one of 'em's worth twenty shilling or more, and there's a dozen of 'em here!"

"Did ye get so much for your gunpowderin', then?"

"No, I didn't get tuppence for that. I did it without pay, along with the militia and some sailors from the King's Yards. A person's got to help save London, it looks like, if he's got two legs to stand on. But I found this little bag o' money today in Cheapside, halfway under some smolderin' wood. In a little while it would've caught fire."

Mrs. Skeet examined the bag. It was made of excellent wool, but was nondescript. "Did you find it near a burnt-out shop, Amos?"

"It was in the open ways, walked o'er and kicked about and ne'er noticed."

"Dear Heaven, ye're rich!"

"I just am," Amos agreed dreamily. "I'll tell Susan tomorrow." He laid his head on the table and fell asleep.

While the Skeets slept, the fire moved closer to Navy Yard, a contingency for which Mr. Pepys had prepared.

So home at night, and find there good hopes of saving our office; but great endeavours of watching all night, and having men ready; and so we lodged them in the office, and had drink and bread and cheese for them.

Never a timid man, Mr. Pepys resolved to sleep at Navy Office, himself, to prevent any treachery.

As he was getting ready to bed down on a quilt, he was furtively accosted by one of the men quartered there. Actually, the man nudged him in the ribs.

"Might I speak personal to ye, sir?" he asked.

"Yes," Mr. Pepys replied tiredly. The office was lighted by the flickering glare of the great fire, and he looked at the man closely, astonished by his fancy waistcoat and neckpiece. "But I can't remember seeing you before," Pepys said. "Were you recruited with these other men?"

"Aye, sir. I be a laborer from the King's Yard at Deptford. I come up with the crowd tonight."

"Speak up, then."

And so Shark spoke up, though in a discreet mumble. "I'd be at fault if I didn't talk, sir, this thing lyin' so heavy on me mind. The way these fires break out, first here, then there— it do seem queer, don't it?"

"It's not natural," Pepys admitted. "We think it's French or Dutch agents. But I'd like to get some sleep, if you don't mind."

"Sleep ye do need, sir. But not till I've told ye this to mull on. Agents could use Lon'on boys fer their devilment."

Pepys looked at him sharply. "Do you have any evidence of it?"

"There's been gutter rats a plenty, sir, in Lon'on this week, an' somethin' points to a perticular little rogue as their leader. I've spotted 'im where 'alf a dozen fires 'ave broke out."

"I thought you came up just tonight from Deptford?"

The rascal hesitated a moment. "I've been on call in the City since Sunday, sir. Only went back to Deptford to get me some rest. Then I be ordered up 'ere to Navy Office."

Samuel Pepys glanced out at the red sky. He distrusted the man, but feared to ignore his story. "You know this boy, you say? You could identify him?"

"I can put me finger on 'im, if ye say the word. He was one

o' the crew that set the Easter Day fires in Aldersgate, but 'e slipped through the net. I swear it."

"What? Why didn't you report this before? Sheriff Sheldon called for informers."

"I often ask mysel' why I didn't, sir. Likely I were too soft. But now, seein' the boy about Lon'on at a time like this, always in the thick o' things, I must speak."

"What's the boy's name?"

"I've got no idee, sir." And the lie deprived Kip Skeet of Mr. Pepys' consideration and protection.

"It's a case for Sheriff Sheldon," Pepys said. "Go to his house and tell him what you've told me. You could be wrong in your deductions, but Sheldon's the one to ferret it out."

Shark went like a streak, and Pepys lay down on Will Hewer's quilt, as far from the sweating, snoring men as possible. He slept till daybreak brought a new alarm. It turned out to be at Bishopsgate, where no fire had been before.

When the laborers returned from extinguishing the fire, Pepys looked for the man who had accosted him last night. He asked for him, describing his waistcoat and neckwear, but none of the men could say what had become of him. None knew his name, or how he had got among them; and this might have struck Samuel Pepys as strange, except that he was so weary.

The Skeet boys were up early Thursday morning and greeted each other warily. Amos fixed his eyes on Kip and considered cuffing him. Kip stepped nimbly out of the way and began to eat his breakfast. Mrs. Skeet, who wanted only peace between her sons, fed them double portions of porridge and filled the air with her scatterbrained chatter.

"Can it be true, as Mr. Hooker says, that Clothworkers' Hall has been afire three days without burnin' down?" Then, not waiting for an answer: "Can I believe my ears that folk are breakin' open butts of sugar and puttin' handfuls in their beer?"

"Yes, Muv," Kip replied. "It's all true."

"You ought to know," Amos said, glaring at Kip. "You live in the City now. Where do you sleep?"

"Anywhere that's handy, dear brother."

"Don't dear brother me, Kip! I've been trying to track you down since Sunday."

"I know you have," Kip said. "I've watched you set off gunpowder. Between jobs you snoop around, lookin' for me."

"Why haven't you shown yourself, then?"

"I didn't want you to yank me home, that's why. I liked what I was doing. I been movin' goods for people, out o' the fire's way."

"You've had practice in that!" Amos shouted. He knew it was unjust, but temper took over his tongue. He had been frightened by Kip's long absence, and now, in reaction, seeing how indifferently Kip treated the matter, he was too angry to control himself. "Yes, you got good practice with Kobet. No wonder you can carry goods out o' smoky houses!"

"What's this?" Mrs. Skeet asked in surprise.

"I won't say it again," Amos replied sullenly.

"No need to," Kip said bitterly. "She heard you."

Mrs. Skeet had, indeed, heard, but it made no sense to her, for the Aldersgate trouble had never reached her ears. It had happened before the Hookers came to live at the wharf, in that era when she heard no gossip. "What day is this?" she asked now.

Kip said he didn't know. Amos thought awhile, said, "It's Thursday."

"And the fire still aburnin'," Mrs. Skeet mourned from the doorway. "Now begins the fifth day. May the Lord send rain."

"I'm going to see Susan now," Amos told them. Then he said to his mother, "It looks like you put my money away?"

"I did, Amos," she assured him. "I climbed up and put it back of those crossed timbers." She pointed out the spot. "I wedged it tight. Is that a fit place?"

"It's all right," Amos said after a moment's hesitation. "I can't think of a better, off hand."

"When will ye be back, son?" Mrs. Skeet asked him anxiously.

"After I've seen Susan I'll be off to the fire again," he told her. "I'll stay all day, likely. But you can count on one thing, Mother, I'll come home to sleep." He looked hard at Kip and added, "Anybody but a knave comes home to sleep."

Kip asked for a third bowl of porridge and ate it, waiting for Amos to get out of sight. Presently he said that he too must return to the City.

"Where do ye aim to go, Kip?" Mrs. Skeet asked him.

"Wherever the fire's about to spread, Muv, that's all I can tell you. But I'll try to come home tonight. I'm real sorry I made you anxious the way I did."

"I was fair out o' my mind with worry, but I forgive ye." She reached into her pocket and took out the coins he had given her, prepared to give them back.

He declined to take more than a shilling, saying it was all he would need. "The rest is for you." But he added ruefully, with a glance at the crossed timbers, "If I heard aright, Amos earned a fistful."

"He don't charge for his services at the fire," Mrs. Skeet said. "But yestiddy he found a little bag o' gold money—ginnies, he called 'em, in Cheapside."

"Whee!" Kip said. The romance of such a thing carried him away. He stood entranced. "Why can't something big happen to me?"

Something big soon did.

An hour later, near Bishopsgate, he was pointed out by Shark to a deputy sheriff and a constable, and they asked him to come along without fuss. Or had he rather wear wrist irons?

"I'll go with you," Kip said in a stunned way. "Where to?"

"Wherever you live," the deputy said. "We'd like to have a few words with your father."

"You can't," Kip replied. "He went down on the *London*."

"Your mother, then. Will she talk to us?"

"She'll talk to you," Kip replied gloomily. And he faced the inevitable and led his captors by the shortest route to Dick's Shore. He was not too alarmed, being unaware of the ugly suspicions surrounding him. He accepted the fact that the Aldersgate trouble had at last caught up with him. Only the time and place of his capture struck him as weird. He thought it funny —almost funny enough to make a boy laugh—that he was being arrested for one fire while attending another.

As they boarded the houseboat, the deputy went ahead, and the constable followed, holding Kip by the arm. No doubt they thought if he intended to bolt, this would be the place he might try it. Mrs. Skeet, just emerging from the cabin, was startled. "What's happened?" she cried out.

"Is this your boy?" the deputy sheriff asked her.

"Yes! It's my youngest."

"He tells us his name's Kip Skeet. Says his dad was a sailor on the *London*."

"And why wouldn't he tell ye so? It's God's truth."

"All right, then. Where's the boy been for the last four days?"

"He's been in the City, attendin' the fire, that's where."

"With your leave?"

"What business is that o' yourn?" Mrs. Skeet asked angrily. "Can't a family have a little disagreement without a badge-wearer comin' to pry?"

"Then I take it, ma'am, the boy's been conducting his shady work without your sanction. So much the better for you. Can you give me an account of his actions on Easter Day?"

"Easter Day? Let's see. . . . All mornin' he was home, nursin' his sick brother. I remember Bow bells a-ringing, and all the other church bells; and I had a beef pudding in the pot, flavored with tansy, which I use if the meat's too strong. After dinner Kip took off to enjoy himself awhile. Do ye object?"

"Do you know where he went, ma'am?"

"It happens I do," said Mrs. Skeet with great satisfaction.

Kip was looking at her in a pleading way, so she hastened to do her honest best. "He told me where he was off to, and it's a respectable place, I can tell ye! He went to Aldersgate Street to see some friends."

"A friend named Kobet, maybe? A boy about seventeen?"

Mrs. Skeet racked her brain, thinking that a remembered acquaintance would benefit Kip's cause, might definitely prove that he was in the good neighborhood specified. She could not know that Kip's beseeching expression meant, "Don't remember!" In a moment she proudly came up with it. "I reckon Kip does have a friend called Kobet. That name has been spoke at this wharf not too long ago. Yes, it has been, though I don't remember the very connection."

"That does it," the deputy said to the constable. "It's what the man swore to. Bring the boy along."

"Where to?" Mrs. Skeet cried out in consternation.

The deputy scratched his chin. "It's a good question, ma'am. Both sheriff prisons are burnt down. Wood Street jail went yesterday; Poultry Compter, the day before. Newgate's burning now."

"It leaves just Bridewell," the constable said.

"Yes. Come on, Skeet. You've got things to tell us. It appears you're in fast company. Like as not, you know some foreign agents that pay boys to set fires. Eh?"

When Mrs. Skeet screamed in protest he said kindly, "Don't take on, ma'am, as if I'd said Bedlam. Bridewell's a decent place, it's a workhouse. His age will be considered."

Kip, dragged ashore, at last understood why he had been arrested for one fire while attending another, and the gravity of his plight engulfed him. Worst of all was his fear that Amos might doubt him. "I've ne'er set a fire, Muv!" he called back shrilly. "You tell Amos I've ne'er set a fire in my life!"

It gladdened Mrs. Skeet's suffering heart to hear this positive denial, for Kip had never been a liar. "I'll tell Amos," she called after them, "and Amos will get ye freed in no time!

Don't lose heart, Kip! We'll use those gold ginnies, to get ye out!"

The deputy sheriff pricked up his ears, hesitated, started to turn back to investigate this new evidence. Then, "Come along, boy. I'll report that."

When he reached the wharf that evening, Amos's first concern was for his brother. "Where's Kip?" he called out as he came aboard the shanty.

"And well ye might ask, Amos!" Mrs. Skeet called in reply, running to meet him. "Your brother was picked up by two men wearin' constables' tall hats, and was brought home fairly early this morn. Then they took him away—to Bridewell, they said!" She wept so loudly that the Hookers heard and seemed about to offer aid.

"Come to the cabin, Mother," Amos said quickly, and drew her after him. "Now tell me!"

Mrs. Skeet began to relate the events and conversations of the morning. She had gotten as far as how she cleverly identified Kobet as an acquaintance when she noticed that her son's face wore a startled look. "Did I do anything wrong?" she asked.

"You oughtn't have acted familiar with the name of Kobet. It puts a burden on us we don't deserve." He rubbed his hand over his eyes as if to clear away some cobwebs. "But no matter," he said. "It had to come out. Kip got in trouble Easter Day in Aldersgate Street, and that chap was the cause of it. Kobet's in prison now for arson and looting."

"Arson? What's that?"

"McTarvish says it's 'the malicious burning of a building.' But Kip's innocent. He did help Kobet get property out of a burnt inn, but he didn't know a gang had set the place on fire. Not till later. Then he gave 'em a wide berth. I'll go to Bridewell tomorrow and tell how Kip got taken in."

"Amos, there's more to it. Wait till ye hear!"

"What do you mean? Is he in another pickle?"

"Those men say Kip has got something to do with London

burnin' down. They think he lights fires for foreign rascals—agents, they're called."

Amos had turned white. "Now see here, Mother—"

"That's what they lay to Kip, Amos! I heard it with my own ears. But Kip was surprised. I could see the wonder in his face, hearin' himself so named. And when they took 'im off, he called back to me, 'Tell Amos I ne'er set a fire in my life!' He said it brave and true. I believed 'im."

"And I believe him," Amos said grimly. "As soon as it's light tomorrow I'll go to Bridewell and tell him so. Then I'll knuckle down to get him cleared."

"I knew I could count on ye, Amos! I called after Kip, to cheer 'im up. 'Amos will get ye freed in no time,' I said. 'Don't lose heart,' I said, 'we'll use those gold ginnies to get ye out!' "

Amos stared at his mother. He was speechless, wondering what damage could come of this. In blabbing at the top of her lungs about his honestly found coins, she had changed them to millstones and hung them about poor Kip's neck. For how else would foreign agents pay but in new English guineas, small in bulk, bright in beauty? Though but six years in circulation, they were handled freely in Holland, in France, in Russia.

"Ye don't look well, Amos. It's best that ye go to bed."

"Just leave me to think a while," he said miserably but gently. He pitied himself as well as Kip. Were two boys ever afflicted with a parent so addlepated? Was there no limit to her idiotic behavior? Must she finally do them in, and herself too?

He slept in his clothes and when dawn came set out for Bridewell to find Kip. It was necessary to make a northerly circuit, for though the great fire was quenched, smoldering ruins and hot ashes made the City's thoroughfares impassable. When he crossed the access to the Great North Road he was interested to observe some soldiers herding a half-dozen men into a heavy wagon drawn by six horses and having painted on its side the words *York Gaol*. He asked a rustic soldier in charge what was going on.

"We be Yorkshire guards sent for to keep order," the soldier said. "We caught these men a-lootin', ecod!"

"What do you aim to do with them?" Amos asked, lingering.

"There's but one prison left standin' in all Lon'on, friend, and it be crowded to the gills. We be about to give the rogues a pretty ride to York."

Amos now made a discovery that caused his heart to leap joyfully. "That one with a guard of his own—" he said, pointing, "the one in irons. Is he something special?"

"He do be, yes. He's just done in his boon companyin. Stabbed his vitals with a kitchen blade to get a gold watch he coveted. There be the bauble he murdered for." The rustic indicated a blanket at the roadside, heaped with jewelry, silver mugs and the like. "Seargent's about to take all the loot to Lord Mayor."

Amos, keeping his hands in his pockets, bent to look at the fateful valuables. The watch in question was bordered with diamonds. "Did you pick out the murderer from hearsay?" Amos wanted to know.

"Ecod, no! Three of us witnessed it, close range. We spied the surprised look on the poor cove's face when he was knifed. He be lyin' in yon garden patch. It's a tidy stabbin', tidy! A surgeon could 'a hardly doon it so weel. Take a look."

"No, thank you, sir," Amos replied politely. "But I'll ask you to take extra notice of your prisoner, there. His name's Shark. He's known for squirmin' out of tight places. Bribery and smooth talk—the one or the other always serves 'im."

"He'll ne'er coom back here, friend. He can't bribe the Yorkshire Guards. He'll be convicted at the next Assizes on our evidence. He'll swing at York. Lon'on's too busy to coddle 'im now."

Amos went thoughtfully on his way. It was not in his nature to relish the picture of the gallows awaiting Shark at grim York Castle. But this accidental knowledge that the evil-intentioned water rat would never again molest them made the day seem less sinister, made his mission to save Kip more promising.

Susan had walked on air after Amos came that Thursday morning and told her of finding the little bag of guineas. At first she had not been able to believe it; she had thought him temporarily out of his head from fighting the fires. But after he had convinced her of the reality of his money, they talked of how to use it.

Might they, perhaps, take a wedding trip to Bristol by stage and stop a few days at an inn? In that case, they would need new luggage, for Susan's portmanteau was shabby, and Amos had never owned a traveling bag. Susan, blushing and laughing, had taught Amos how to write *Mr. and Mrs. Amos Skeet, London,* so he could sign the tavern register.

The possibility of finding the owner of the guineas was remote, they felt. Nor did it bother them much; the area where the bag had lain was in the path of fleeing merchants and goldsmiths; to such persons, perhaps, the loss would seem trifling. Their final decision had been to use the money—if unclaimed—to buy furnishings for their future lodgings in Stepney. "With a chest of drawers for you to keep your things in," Amos had declared generously, "and a little sewing box."

"But first some new clothes for you, love!" Susan had insisted. "And a shaving stand, like Mr. Pepys'!"

Their hastily snatched kisses had been the sweeter for their having offered each other these extravagant gifts. Moreover, Amos was in a good mood because of Kip's return home after his four-day absence; and because the fire seemed to be under control, and those fighting it could soon rest from their efforts.

All in all, it had been a beautiful morning visit, even though Luce had wandered in and out, complaining of the food shortage.

But that was the last time Susan saw Amos for many days.

She was puzzled, but the aftermath of the fire kept her from having any leisure in which to brood. The Pepys possessions were scattered in so many places that it was a gigantic task to put them together again. First, the cellar had to be readied for the money chests. Then, wainscoting and floors must be scrubbed upstairs and down by Susan and Luce. Decorators —Pepys called them carpenters—were called in to set up the beds and bookcases and to hang draperies and pictures. Finally, when the smoke had abated, brass and silver and windows must be polished.

Pepys wrote on Saturday, September 22nd: *My house is so clean as I never saw it, or any other house in my life, and everything in as good condition as before the fire.*

But, by now, Susan was so beset with anxiety that she decided to go to Dick's Shore to see what had happened to Amos.

On Sunday afternoon, tired as she was, she set out to walk the distance. For all her courage, the burnt streets and gaping cellars dismayed her, so her joy was twofold when she met Amos at Bishopsgate, on his way to her. They went, hand in hand, to the ruins in Crutched Friars. That place seemed strangely orderly, after the newer, rawer ruins of the City.

Amos seemed so distraught, so unlike himself, that Susan dreaded to ask him what the matter was. Finally, to get him started, she inquired, "Is it Kip?"

"Yes. Kip's in Bridewell. He was taken there the day I came to see you."

"Was it the Aldersgate trouble?"

"That and more." He told her all the circumstances of Kip's arrest. He said that he had not yet seen Kip, though more than two weeks had passed and he had gone often to Bridewell. Furthermore, nobody in authority would bother to talk to him—neither magistrates, clerks, nor jailors.

"Oh, Amos, how sad! Could Kip think you've abandoned him?"

"No," Amos said, brightening, "he gets word from me by way of a guard that I pay. And he sends me ordinary messages the same way. I'm sure the messages come from Kip himself, because there's always something in 'em that nobody else would know about. One time he asked about Singer's sore paw. Next time, he asked about a customer we sell herring to—things like that. But we haven't dared do any connivin'. Not yet. There's no use making the guard suspicious. It might go hard with Kip."

"Yes, Amos, wait till you've worked something out," Susan advised. "Kip knows you're trying to help him."

"But I've not made any headway, Susan. Nothing's done regular now. Kip's trial was over and done before I could get there."

"Do you mean they've already passed sentence?"

"You could call it that. They're going to detain 'im, is all I know. Sunday a week ago I got this message from Kip: 'Nokes' Dock will have to bow to me now, because I'm a King's Ward.'"

"What did that gibberish mean, Amos?"

"I had no idea, so I went to McTarvish at Lime House and asked him what was meant. He said the Crown can take over troublesome boys—orphans, usually—and confine 'em till they're fourteen years of age. He says it appears they've taken over Kip, regardless of his being already fourteen and having a living parent and an adult brother. He says they seem to think Kip's dangerous."

"Amos, you must do something!"

"I mean to try, Susan. But those guineas of mine are heavy against 'im. Blast it, if my mother had just held her tongue!"

Susan did not reply, for fear she would denounce the woman to her own son as the world's worst busybody. So she sat demurely still and imagined herself shaking Mrs. Skeet till her teeth chattered. It was a great pleasure.

"McTarvish says Kip's lucky in one way," Amos said, cheerful again. "The King's Wards have been housed in a stinking dormitory at Poultry Compter, that jail near the poultry vats, and they had to smell wet feathers all day. But Poultry burned. The inmates are at Bridewell now. McTarvish says Bridewell's spacious and it gets better air, being up river. He said Bridewell used to be a royal palace."

"Yes," Susan said, "it's a part of St. Bride's parish. I could see its towers from where I lived. But Mother never let me go near it because of the rough people that came and went, to see the inmates."

"They're rougher than ever now," Amos said gloomily. "All the Newgate prisoners are quartered there since the fire. That's why I can't get at Kip, McTarvish thinks. He says Bridewell rules are tightened, likely, to keep the Newgate felons from escaping."

"Things will soon be better, love," Susan promised stoutly. "I'll beg Mr. Pepys to use his influence and get him freed. He'll know how to do it. He goes to Bridewell workhouse often, to get the Navy's flags made."

"He'll know how to do it, but *will* he? Old Pepys looks mighty flinty to me. I'd sooner ask Admiral Penn."

"The one or the other," Susan replied. She put her arms about Amos and caressed him as if he were her child who needed reassuring. That must be her role now; to soothe him, to keep him from some impulsive act that might imperil Kip and himself too. She did not want this role. She would have preferred being just an engaged girl, waiting for her wedding day.

Kip and the other King's Wards were, indeed, fortunate to have some pleasant work to do: making flags for the Navy. And in their leisure time they could look through the barred windows and see the busy Thames River. For the workhouse was in New Bridewell, directly on the water (once foreshore), a quadrangle built to the front of the old. The boys enjoyed their surveys of the river more than their liberty (so called) in the courtyard, where nothing could be seen but sky and scudding clouds overhead, and four stone walls enclosing them. Those walls had barred windows against which faces pressed

—some evil, some tragic, some resigned—to peer out at them at play.

The healthy young can adjust to difficult changes; and so it was with Kip. That he was in captivity, unjustly accused of an ugly crime, dismayed and saddened him, but it did not destroy him. He expected to be cleared and released, and he was especially hopeful after he had made contact with Amos. His brother would think of a way.

Amos's messages cheered him greatly. They were brought to him by a dour old guard of the King's Wards named Ephraim, a man who had been in Cromwell's army and was a true Roundhead—as the Puritans were called—in his love of the Old Testament. He had memorized much of The Proverbs and always announced chapter and verse when quoting.

His favorite saying went thus: "Proverbs Seventeen, three: The firing pot is for silver, and the furnace for gold; but the Lord trieth the hearts."

He would utter those words in a carrying voice when he saw a boy looking unduly dejected. In most cases the sermon fell on deaf ears, but Kip bothered to figure out what the old chap meant. If your troubles were great, then God was trying your courage. He considered you more important than gold and silver, He attended to you personally.

Another quotation which Ephraim used one day was truly fitting. "Proverbs Fourteen, thirty," he intoned. "A sound heart is the life of the flesh; but envy is the rottenness of the bones." That was aimed at some of the King's Wards who were looking with consuming envy at a discharged ward mate about to go out into the world of freedom. No doubt Kip's face was the most covetous of all, for the old Puritan shook a warning finger at him.

One Sunday afternoon Ephraim called Kip aside and announced in gentler tones than usual, "Proverbs Seventeen, seventeen: A friend loveth at all times, and a brother is born for adversity."

"Do you mean my brother's here again?" Kip asked eagerly.

"Aye, boy. He says to inform ye that he and your mother be in good health. Your dog caught two partridge when he took him to run in Rolfe Fields this morn. Lime House has ne'er started up its kilns since the fire, he says, and he now works at removing rubble in the City. The end of his message has a tricky sound, boy, and I hold back my tongue from bringing it to ye. I surmise a hidden meaning."

"Mr. Ephraim, do you think it's right to surmise?"

"What, boy?"

"Ain't surmisin' just suspectin' without proof? When our mother says 'I surmise,' Amos and me don't take to it. 'I surmise ye've been fightin' again,' she'll say. Or, 'I surmise ye haven't cleaned the fish tubs all week.' She's usually wrong."

The old guard looked troubled. "There be a verse in Timothy somewhere about evil surmisings," he mused. "Yes, there do be, though I'm not cozy enough in the New Testament to bring it up."

He went away, leaving Kip feeling anxious and defeated. But after several turns around the big stone chamber he returned and said, "The rest of your brother's message be this. 'Mr. Pepys has promised Susan to look into things.'"

"Thank you, sir! Kindly tell my brother I'm glad to hear all this news. Tell 'im I hope Mr. Pepys won't forget."

"I'll tell him for ye. I take a little money from your brother to deliver these messages, because I need to eke out my pay. But I'd ne'er do anything to defeat the Crown's purpose. I'd not ferment a plot, not for any price. Do ye understand?"

"Oh, yes, Mr. Ephraim." Kip went back to his work, hacking cotton cloth for flags. Now we're getting somewhere, he thought joyfully as he plied his shears. He knew Mr. Pepys to be a fast stepper, a man who got things done.

And Pepys did busy himself for Kip at once. For Susan had told the boy's story so touchingly, and Amos had filled in the details so straightforwardly that he could not have done otherwise unless he had had a heart of stone. Such a heart Samuel Pepys did not have. Though all too often he was selfish and deceitful in his dealings, he could be touched by another's woe.

He felt concern because of Susan's distress, and because he knew himself to have had a part in his former fish boy's arrest. He told Amos of the circumstances, describing the glib laborer in the flashy waistcoat who had been quartered in Navy Office, and had informed on a boy he declined to name.

"The man was Shark, an enemy of ours," Amos said. "It couldn't have been another. He wants Kip and me out of the way because he craves our houseboat. Now that houses are so scarce, he's hard after it, I reckon."

"But there was a good deal of truth in what the rogue told me," Pepys reminded Amos. "Your brother *was* involved in that Aldersgate trouble, you've admitted as much. It was a mighty bad matter. I attended the trials."

"Yes, sir. But it's like I told you. Kip was taken in. He wasn't shrewd to what went on—not like Montagu and those others."

"At least you believe that, I see." Mr. Pepys was not so sure, himself, for by nature he was a suspicious man. If a Montagu could be a juvenile criminal, why couldn't a wharf boy? But he would go to Bridewell and investigate. It appeared that Skeet had lacked proper defense.

Samuel Pepys had a talent for combining business with pleasure. He might buy a book in Westminster after making a report on Tangier. He might have his viol strung while on his way to inspect rope at Blackwall. To satisfy his curiosity he would go miles out of his way to examine a rare shrub in a friend's garden, or to attend an experiment in blood transfusion at Gresham College. He incited people to conversation; and while he listened attentively to dukes and admirals, he could be just as taken with the remarks of a clever child or a simple old man. "How ingenious!" he would say, quoting them to his wife. "How innocent!"

He especially enjoyed going to Bridewell, where he met "all sorts."

Several years ago he had arranged to have the Navy's flags made at the workhouse, at a saving to the Crown, and it was his business to buy the India calico out of which they were constructed. The cloth came in lengths of twenty-five yards, called, for some reason, bewpers. A surprising number of ensigns were needed for England's fighting ships and merchantmen. The salt spray faded their bright colors, and the wind whipped them to shreds. The flags were made at long tables by the children of imprisoned debtors and vagrants. A *pretty sight*, Pepys wrote of it.

On the morning of Pepys' special visit to Bridewell he went first to the trial chamber, to seek out the magistrates who had sentenced Kip. But here was confusion. Because of the recent gutting of Old Bailey (London's courthouse), the King's Benchers were sitting at Bridewell, forcing the magistrates of lesser courts to try their cases where they could.

Pepys looked for, and found, the chief magistrate who used to conduct trials at the sheriff court in Poultry Compter. His fellows had departed, and he was tidying his table. The man wore neither judge's wig nor robe, and he was rather scrubby, Pepys thought. He wondered if he were fit to decide the fate of boys in serious trouble.

Pepys introduced himself. He told the man he had come to look into the case of Kip Skeet, a Dick's Shore boy, accused of setting fires. "Do you remember him?"

"Most assuredly. I remember him very well. We made him a King's Ward, directly we got hold of him. He's here with the other boys from Poultry jail."

"I know he's here, and I've come to see about his release. Or, anyway, a new trial for him. He's fourteen years old. He has an adult brother, not to say a mother in honest trade. Under the circumstances, he can't be held as a King's Ward."

"Mayhap not." The man measured his words, and Pepys saw that he was not stupid; he was a magistrate on his way up. "But he can be removed from the scene, and he must be.

London is now afraid of fire. A young arsonist is as dreaded as an old one."

"What you say would apply if he were guilty," Pepys answered. "But it appears this boy is innocent." And he told Kip's story. The magistrate listened to the end, then:

"Mr. Pepys, I've heard of you, of course. You stand high. Why do you concern yourself with young Skeet?"

Pepys could not bring himself to say, "Because I'm sometimes soft," for it was not in keeping. So he gave the other reason. "My kitchen maid is pledged to his brother."

"And she can hardly do her work, for fretting?"

"That's so," Pepys admitted with a laugh.

"But a good many people would fret more if this boy were turned loose." The magistrate went to a cupboard, opened it with a key, hunted through a sheaf of papers, and came out with one page, closely written over. "Here's his record, Mr. Pepys, as sworn to by his accuser, a man that works at the King's Yard at Deptford."

"Did you get his name, by the way?"

For the first time the magistrate seemed unsure of his ground. "I must have got it, yet I failed to record it. He signed with an X, being unable to write. Maybe the name will come to me."

"If it does," Pepys said, "disregard it. It's apt to be spurious. The knave's known as Shark. He needs to maneuver the Skeet boys out of his way. He's got designs on their shanty boat. As far as I'm concerned, that makes his testimony worthless."

"But no new fires sprang up, Mr. Pepys, after this boy was brought in. Think on that."

Pepys thought on it, puzzled afresh.

"Furthermore, Mr. Pepys, there's the matter of the little bag of guineas you've brushed aside so lightly—the money that was reported to us by the deputy sheriff. The boy himself admits of its existence in his house, but says his brother found the bag in Cheapside."

"And so he did," Pepys replied. "I told you so in plain

English. The sum comes to between twelve and thirteen pounds."

"Did you witness the finding, Mr. Pepys?"

"No," said Pepys impatiently, "of course not. But Amos Skeet has told me the circumstances. He's one of the most reliable boys you could hope to find. Really stanch, Magistrate. I can get you character vouchers from Captain Marsh of the Lime House, and from one Nokes, who owns the Dick's Shore herring sheds."

"A reliable boy, you say. Stanch. Just the sort to protect a younger brother he doted on. Have you thought on that?"

"No, I haven't, Magistrate."

"Here's another thing, Mr. Pepys. Young Skeet managed to get a man out of Bedlam. On Easter Day, just prior to the Aldersgate trouble, he passed a coat and hat through the fence to an inmate."

"Because the inmate lacked clothing, no doubt."

"Clothing for escape, yes. When confronted with this accusation, the said Kip Skeet replied to us, 'I did it so the man could walk away. He didn't belong there.' You can see the confession here on this paper, accurately writ down by my clerk. Look, please."

Pepys looked, shrugged in bewilderment. "That's something I'd not heard about."

"Our informer had followed up that case. The escaper was Nath Sunday, a laborer highly useful to Bedlam; a stonemason, a layer of tiles, an all-round handy man."

"He couldn't have been a madman, then."

"His family had him committed 'for the public safety,' it says here. Who are we to set up a contrary opinion?"

"I'm more confused than when I came here," Samuel Pepys admitted. "I hardly feel sure of anything now."

"When we magistrates feel unsure, Mr. Pepys, we can't shrug it off. We've decided to send the boy to Jamaica on the next ship going out. Some of the other King's Wards will go, too, for we're badly crowded here. We think it's the best solution. The King needs colonizers in the Indies."

"Cane cutters, you mean," Pepys spat out. "Admiral Penn spent some time out there with the Fleet. He said hardly one English boy in four survived the fevers. He said many of his strongest sailors were jaundiced, and died. That's one reason we can't get enlistments, he thinks; they dread the Indies."

"That's a gloomy view, Mr. Pepys. Conditions out there are better lately."

"Let us hope," Pepys said. He was no longer uncertain of his feelings in the case of the City versus Kip Skeet. "I'll go look in at the workhouse now. Good day, Magistrate."

He went at once to the New Bridewell factories and addressed himself to Mr. Poyntz, Master of Workhouse. "I want to see how the flags are coming on," he said. "Is the yardage holding out?"

"We'll need a hundred yards of white calico, sir, before another week's past."

"What?" Pepys said, laughing. "Is the entire Fleet surrendering again?" It was their standard joke. "By the way, Mr. Poyntz, I'd like a few words with one of your guards, a man named Ephraim, if he's on duty."

"He's in there with the King's Wards, Mr. Pepys. You'll find him quoting Proverbs, like as not. He's a kind man, Ephraim is, and a reliable guard."

Pepys inspected the sewing tables with his usual critical eye. Whenever he noticed a piece of color ill-applied, he called the child's attention to it. "Rip it off and sew it again," he would instruct, for he detested a lopsided ensign. The little workers did their best, he knew, what with frostbit fingers and never enough for breakfast, and he would always end his visits by tossing them coins, for a scramble. He was courteous to the gaunt women who supervised, the debtors' wives, though they were never as exacting as he could have wished.

At a cutting table he found Kip Skeet. He recognized him by his resemblance to Amos, and by his eager, "Good day, Mr. Pepys!"

"Well, Skeet," Pepys said, "I'm sorry to see you here."

"Amos says—" began Kip, waving his shears excitedly.

"This is not the time to discuss it," Pepys headed him off. Actually, he was in a quandary. He did not want to tell the boy he had tried and failed. Nor did he dare, impetuous though he was, advise him to escape from here the best way he could, and quickly. "I have you in mind, Kip," he said. "Let it go at that."

"Yes, sir," Kip answered, crestfallen.

Pepys went to the old guard and drew him aside. He introduced himself and told of his position as Clerk of the Acts of the Admiralty. He managed, in an offhand way, to get in a good word for the late Oliver Cromwell. "When I was a student at Cambridge I was something of a Roundhead," he admitted. "I used to shout for him, after ale. But Cromwell's dead now, and I serve the Stuarts. I serve them the best I can, for my country's good."

"And so do I, sir, wastrels though they be."

"Rulers come and go, Ephraim, but there'll always be an England."

"Aye, that's the way I see it, too."

With this rapport established between them, Pepys mentioned his connection with Bridewell—the manufacture of the flags. "Formerly there were only the inmates' children in this workshop," he said. "That was before they moved the King's Wards to Bridewell. They're a dejected-looking group, I must say."

"Aye, sir, they're a sad lot. Poultry Compter dampened 'em."

"I'm interested in a new boy with the Wards—Kip Skeet. His brother has asked my help. What sort of charge is young Skeet, I wonder? Does he give you trouble?"

"Ne'er much trouble, sir. He's a bright, kind boy; prankish, is all. And a cut above most of the Wards."

"Would you favor his being shipped to Jamaica?"

"God forbid, sir! He's only here on suspicion."

"Then I'll get to the point," Pepys said, and he motioned the guard to a spot where they could not be overheard. "The boy is innocent of the serious charges against him. He's done an impulsive act or two, and he's been used by some bad citizens in a conspicuous way. But it's my belief he's been punished enough. He's got a reliable brother to watch out for him, as you very well know, Ephraim. But first he must be delivered. Kindly let Kip Skeet walk out of this prison this evening as if he were the son of a vagrant confined here—one of those children who come and go. Otherwise he'll end in the Islands, a total waste."

"Are ye certain about Jamaica?"

"As certain as taxes. I've just learned it. Some of the other Wards will go, too. It's to ease the crowded conditions here."

"With some it mayn't matter too much," the old guard mused. "They've got no kin, no future. But Skeet has got family ties. It's pitiful news ye've brought me."

"There was a boy I neglected to help once," Pepys confessed. "I don't fancy a second dish of it."

The guard stood stonily still, thinking. As well he might, for he valued his position.

"Well, Ephraim?" Pepys said, looking at his watch.

"I agree, sir. But I'd ne'er do it for pay. Proverbs Thirteen, seven and eight: There is he that maketh himself rich, yet hath nothing. There is he that maketh himself poor, yet hath great riches. The ransom of a man's life are his riches. . . . The ransom of a *boy's* life in this case."

"Well put, Mr. Ephraim," Pepys said. "And tell the boy to hide out in Whitefriars. I'll send his brother to find him." He left then, not intending to become any more involved than need be.

That evening when the sun's rays no longer lighted the big stone chamber, the old guard told the women to clear the tables. "Then count the shears," he ordered, "and write down the figures. Do the same for measuring rules and needles. They've not been counted in a week. And ye, Skeet, stay to help. Ye've been restless today. I'll get some work out o' ye, yet."

"Yes, Mr. Ephraim," Kip answered, surprised.

The old guard took his King's Wards, excepting Kip, to their dormitory, where they would stay locked in till suppertime, that being the customary procedure.

When he returned he inspected and checked. At Kip's table he fumbled fussily. "I thought ye were a good writer of figures," he complained. "Ye said a Scotchman taught ye. But see here, I can't hardly tell a six from a nine." Then, in a low voice, serenely determined, "Go out with the workhouse children and get ye lost. Mr. Pepys said as much. Abide in Whitefriars, he instructed. He'll send your brother to find ye. Ye're marked for Jamaica, boy, and soon."

Kip was stunned, never having thought of exile. He had become reconciled to serving awhile in Bridewell, if such must be his lot, and then returning home, somewhat branded by his record. Being innocent, he would live it down. Often during the tedious hours at the cutting table, and even at recreation in the courtyard, he had speculated on his future in this way. Not once had he considered the dreaded West Indies.

"If I could go to Dick's Shore just for tonight—" Kip begged. "It looks like I've got to see Amos!"

"Stay away from your home, Skeet, or ye'll get your brother in serious trouble. Mark ye this. Whitefriars—Alsatia, it's called—is near here, over beyond Salisbury Court. In the old days, folk in trouble fled there; and the White Friars—an order that's gone now—took them in. A sanctuary, it was called. It's now a nuisance to the City. Criminals go there and settle down. Constables never enter. It's a cutthroat sort of place, but ye'll be all right if ye don't meddle. Make no chums. Confide in none. There's inns, of a sort. Do ye still have the ten shillin' your brother sent ye?"

"Nine of 'em. I gave one away."

"Go now, with the others. Tomorrow I'll have to report ye

missing." He bent over the cotton yardage and recounted the bewpers, as if some rolls had escaped him. He remained thus engrossed until the room was empty and still.

Kip went out with the workshop children, most of them younger than himself, and he was glad of his short stature. None noticed him; not even the women scattered among them, perhaps for being too weary. But it was his fate, as he went along the last passage, to meet Kobet, whom he had not seen in all those weeks. And Kobet was with some criminals under guard, going to recreation in one of the courtyards.

Kip pretended not to see him, but Kobet would have none of it. He blocked Kip's way. "Look who's with the little flag toilers!" he exclaimed. "Pip Squeak, of all people! Do you live near here, Pip?"

The rowdies laughed, and Kip turned an angry red. "You know my name's not that!" he said to Kobet. "You know it's Kip Skeet. Shut up, and let me by."

The guard jerked Kobet into line again, and Kip hurried past. He merged with a workhouse family, pretending to be one of them, and so left Bridewell at its main gate, under the unsuspecting eyes of four helmeted guards.

He kept at the heels of this family, a woman and three children dressed in brown homespun smocks. Because of their short hair and bleak attire, the sex of the children was undefined. Kip was pleased to find that they were going west, possibly to Salisbury Court. If so, he would have coverage most of the way.

He was sorry that he had blurted out his identity there in the passage. But anger had caused it. The sight of Kobet had infuriated him, for Kobet was at the root of his troubles. And for Kobet to sneer at him and make laughing stock of his name had been more than he could stand.

The workhouse family, poor as they were, had a dwelling, and Kip watched them enter it, enviously. It was in one of the shabbier lanes of Salisbury Court. The woman, opening a ground-floor door with a key that she had, shooed her brood within and closed the door. If she had seen Kip, she gave no thought to him, being engrossed with how to keep her family while her husband was in durance. To such persons, the problem was a vicious circle. If a man broke, as the saying went, his creditors had him imprisoned; and if imprisoned, how could he pay his debts?

Kip must now walk alone, and he continued in the alley, going west. This brought him out in Water Lane, a steep and rocky thoroughfare running from Fleet Street to the Thames River. There was a man coming toward him from Fleet Street. In the purposeful way he moved, in the way he handled his cane, and in the height of his hat, he suggested a constable or a firewarden making his rounds. Kip felt a bitterness toward fate. Just over there was Whitefriars, and he dare not cross Water Lane and enter the area while the man was in sight. He had no choice but to keep close to the walls and go toward the river.

Presently Kip came to a house so tall and narrow and steep that he looked up at it with his mouth agape. And while he was staring upward, a very old woman in a nightcap was staring down from four stories above, just as fixedly.

"Is that you, Tom?" she called in a quavering voice.

Kip did not answer, so she tried again. "If it's you, Tom, take the key from under the waterspout and go it. Sweep the cellar and polish the pewter. Dust the cupboards with the turkey wing. Your bread and cheese is on the cobble bench. Do you hear me, Tom, or be you another boy?"

In a glad flash Kip remembered his christening, and Amos's, a vague occurrence at a time of sorrow that rarely came to his mind. The old clergyman at Lea Roads had named them both Thomas, after their father.

"I'm Thomas," he replied loudly. "Who else would I be?"

"Enter, then, and do the char work. The family's gone, and I've got a sprained foot."

"Yes, ma'am," Kip called blithely up to her. "Don't bother

about a thing, ma'am," and he scrambled for the key under the waterspout.

The man had now caught up with him and had slowed his pace, to observe. He was a constable, for he wore the badge. Kip thought it wise to continue his conversation with the remote old woman, letting her instructions fall on him like gentle rain from heaven. "If the pewter polish gives out, ma'am," he shouted, "can I use sand and vinegar?"

"It won't give out, Tom! Go in and quit quibbling."

The constable, satisfied, moved on.

Kip fitted the big key in the lock and turned it. The door was of heavy black oak on ancient hinges, but it swung open under his hand. He closed it behind him and locked it from within, sighing with relief.

The cellar was spacious, with a hard earth floor. While it had a door and high windows on Water Lane, its three other sides were blank masonry walls, built into the hillside. Against one wall a stairway mounted to the floor above. Kip now knew this to be the "Hanging Sword," an old house that Susan had once described to him as a thing of curiosity.

Everything was as the old lady had implied. The floor needed sweeping. A rush broom was at hand, and also a turkey wing that had seen hard service. Pewter dishes and candlesticks were stacked on a table, waiting to be cleaned. There was a crock of metal polish, with some rags beside it. Drinking water was in a large jug. Bread and cheese and a red apple were in a basket on the cobbling bench.

"Whee!" Kip exulted. He was very thirsty, for water at Bridewell was sparingly allotted. Besides, his escape had produced an added thirst, as if his body were dried in the salt of anxiety. He drank deeply from the water jug. Then he gratefully devoured the food set out for the char boy who had not come.

It was almost dark. Kip lighted a pair of stumpy candles with some sulphur matches and began to clean the pewter. His right hand was blistered from working the shears at Bridewell, but he did not let it deter him. For no reason, he felt, could he fail the old woman in the nightcap, his unwitting hostess.

That job handsomely done, he wielded the turkey wing on everything in sight, and swept the floor, scudding the trash into a coalbin. He was tired and sleepy past belief, and it seemed only reasonable for him to spend the night. There was an old quilt in one of the cupboards. He shook it out and made a bed on the floor and slept sweetly.

When morning came, he let himself out with skill and caution and hid the key where he had found it, under the waterspout. Then he crossed Water Lane and entered White-friars—sometimes called Alsatia—London's worst slum.

When Mr. Pepys left Bridewell he hurried home and told Susan what he had learned, and what he had done. He was careful that no one overheard. For he, a faithful servant of the Royal Navy and an honorary member of the Clothworkers' Company, had thwarted both the Crown and the City in help-ing a King's Ward to escape.

But now he was washing his hands of the matter.

"Go to Nokes' wharf," he instructed Susan, "and tell Amos to be on the lookout for his brother. I recommended White-friars, so I suppose Kip will go there. Tell Amos to get the boy out of London. Otherwise, he'll be picked up again, and I'll not lift a finger. If young Skeet lands in the West Indies now, be it on his brother's head."

Susan got into her wraps, excited and frightened. "Suppose Amos is not at home, Mr. Pepys?"

"Then stay till he comes, if it's all night." He went to tell Mrs. Pepys he had given Susan Stokes his permission to visit her sweetheart. And he silently bore her reproaches for his interference in the kitchen.

Susan had sought many an excuse to be with Amos, but she found herself dreading this meeting as something hard and inevitable. It seemed unfair that she must be the one to tell him Kip was marked for Jamaica: she had heard it said that people turned against those bringing them bad news. She would have lagged, if she had dared; but knowing that every hour counted, she hurried. It had rained last night, making the cluttered ways slippery underfoot. Once she fell to her knees, soiling her coat and gloves.

Mrs. Skeet was surprised and pleased to see her. She took the coat and sponged it. "Did somebody push ye?" she asked.

"No, Mrs. Skeet. I hurried too fast."

"Oh, ye're on an errand, then?"

"Mr. Pepys gave me some time off when I wasn't expecting it," she evaded. "When will Amos get home?"

"I don't know, Susan. He's clearing rubble, as ye know. He works on Thames Street now, where the warehouses burned. I tell ye, Susan, I'm used to Amos being agone, but the way I miss Kip is pitiful. Since that boy's been in Bridewell, this wharf ain't the same, at least not to me and Amos and Singer."

"I'm sure of that, Mrs. Skeet," Susan replied nervously. She let the poor woman talk her heart out, not replying except with murmurs of sympathy. Wild horses could not have dragged out of her the latest news of Kip Skeet; for whatever Kip's hazard, his mother could be counted on to make it worse.

When Amos approached the dock, Susan saw him coming, and she surprised Mrs. Skeet by snatching up her coat and running to meet him. Amos kissed her, but apprehensively.

"Come for a walk with me, Amos," she begged. "Come right now."

"All right, Susan." He was sure she had news of Kip, or she would not be pestering him to take a walk when he was tired and dirty and headed for home.

She held to his arm, and they trudged toward the Lime House. As quickly as she could she told him that Mr. Pepys had not been able to get Kip's release, or even a new trial for him. She told about Jamaica, word for word as Pepys had told it to her. She told of the plan to let Kip walk away from

Bridewell, which would almost surely be accomplished that evening. She said Kip must stay in Whitefriars till he, Amos, could send him out of London.

Amos's jaw had tightened, his feet moved more slowly. Finally he stood stock-still. "So Kip's free this very night," he said. He was taking the cheerful view, already reaching for a solution.

"What will we do, Amos?" Susan asked. "Can you find him before he's captured?"

"I think so, Susan. Kip's cute to take care of himself."

"But after that, Amos?"

"I don't know. I'll have to ask McTarvish."

Ahead of them loomed Captain Marsh's old timbered house; and a little distance from it, the office and the kilns. "Come with me, Susan," Amos said. "McTarvish lives at the office because his wife died. "You can hear the talk between us. I need to ask him how to take Kip to America."

"Whatever are you saying, Amos?"

"McTarvish advised America. As soon as he heard of Kip's trouble, he spoke out for getting him there. He says London's not the place for a boy now. 'London's been whipped to its knees twice now,' is the way he put it—the plague, then the fire. It'll take London a long time to recover, he thinks. For them that haven't got money and patience, he says, it's the wrong place. Kip's not got either."

"But did you say you needed to *take* Kip there, Amos? Did I hear you aright?"

"You heard me aright, Susan. What would Kip do without me?"

What will *I* do without you? Susan thought rebelliously.

McTarvish received them in his office, laying aside some geometry he was absorbed in.

"Mr. McTarvish," Amos said, "this is Susan Stokes that you've heard me speak of, the girl I'm going to marry."

When? thought Susan bitterly. *Where?*

McTarvish greeted Susan with reserve, not warming to her,

for he thought Amos had been caught and given the bit too young. (He had once said to Amos, "We Scots marry later than the English, because we're cannier.")

"Sit down, Susan," he said, and dusted off a chair for her. "Well, Amos, you look edgy. Have you news of Kip?"

"Yes, sir. He's marked for Jamaica on the first ship going out. But he's escaping tonight from the workhouse, we hear, with the help of an old guard—that man Ephraim. And forget his name, sir."

"May I be struck by lightning if I speak it."

"Kip will hide out in Whitefriars, Mr. McTarvish. My job is to find him before Bridewell does."

"Well said, Amos. Time matters now."

"Will you read me that letter again, sir? The last one from that doctor across the water? I'd like Susan to hear it."

McTarvish nodded, got rid of some snuff, took a letter from his pocket, unfolded it.

"Esteemed friend, McTarvish," he read in a confidential drone, the customary style of a Scot with a letter to share. "Your remarks on the great horrid plague interest me greatly, especially the part played by quicklime in preventing the spread of the evil. I will use the knowledge against a contagion striking the colonies, which God forbid."

McTarvish got up and opened a shutter to let in more light, and Susan noticed some cobwebs. An unwashed dish, as well. She pitied him, having no wife to keep him tidy.

He resumed the letter. "I faithfully practice medicine and surgery up and down the Delaware River. But this country is so remarkable that a professional man can hardly resist making money on the side. I have a small tannery, and we are exporting our beaver skins to England, also some lesser hides. But our problem is getting boys to work for us, every one wanting to strike out for himself before he is dry behind the ears. If you know any reliable lads, recommend that they come to this place and apply. They can expect steady work and kind treatment."

"That interests me, sir," Amos interrupted feelingly.

Susan sat silent. McTarvish nodded and resumed:

"Our settlement is composed of English and Swedish peoples, all busy getting ahead. The climate is good. The native Red Men are friendly. I prefer this place to New York, a wee bit north of us, though the latter has a splendid harbor. Ships reach us by entering Delaware Bay and ascending the river. We are located just where the Delaware River receives the Schuylkill River. My tannery is thereabout." McTarvish folded the paper and returned it to his pocket. "The rest is personal. That's the gist of John McKnight's letter."

"What's the name of the settlement, sir?" Amos asked.

"I've wondered that, myself," McTarvish admitted. And a name the place must lack until Admiral Penn's eccentric son William would arrive and dub it Philadelphia, City of Brotherly Love.

"If people are to go there," Susan complained, "it ought at least have a name. How else would they find it?"

"If you were listening to the letter, Susan, you must have noticed that he located the place exactly. It's where the Schuylkill River joins the Delaware."

"But how would you send a letter?" Susan persisted.

"Dr. John McKnight, Delaware River in America, is how I address him. I always give my letter to a ship's master in person, one who's about to make the crossing."

"I see," Susan said, biting her lower lip. "It all sounds very well. But maybe your friend is overpraising the settlement, just to get boys to leave London and work for him at low wages."

"Lass," thundered McTarvish, "I've known the McKnights of Dumfriesshire all my life, and there's ne'er been a liar in the lot!" He took snuff and glared at her.

Amos was shocked by the ill will between McTarvish and Susan, and he saw that the Scot's harshness had brought tears to Susan's eyes. He took her hand and pressed it, to reassure her.

"About Kip, sir," he said. "If he gets safely out of Bridewell, and if I find him before he's run down, I mean to take him to that settlement! It sounds like a fit place, to me. We could both work at the tannery. I'd find lodgings. Susan and my mother could join us next summer."

"Oh?" Susan blinked through her tears, as alert as a squirrel that has just heard an acorn fall. The Delaware River that had been so menacing was now alluring.

"Must you burden yourself so soon, Amos?" McTarvish bellowed. He considered women to be nuisances, for his late wife had been a scold—a woman who objected to his books, his mathematics, his choice of food and drink, his snuff, and the way he filled the coal scuttle. His married daughter was like her mother; she nagged her husband, a Parliament clerk, until he could not call his very boots his own. No wonder poor McTarvish recommended a season of bachelorhood.

"Amos," he said persuasively, "I speak for your own good, and for Kip's. A young chap works better in single harness when he's getting a start in life. Make no promises to this lass and your mother as to when they can come to you. Indeed, I doubt the wisdom of your mother's going out to America at all. Kip has told me how she tries the both of you, him and you. Let her keep her boat and her trade. You've told me Shark's been netted fast in York prison—he's no longer a menace to her. Send her money when need be, but leave her moored."

Susan was outraged. "Mrs. Skeet tries her sons terribly, sir, it's true. But she loves them, and they return it. She's a weak, flighty soul, as I suppose you know. She's easily led to drink rum. If she were left here, lonesome and without anything to live for, she might make a wreck of her life."

"That's true, sir," Amos said. "And I love Susan the more for pointing out my plain duty."

McTarvish threw up his hands to show defeat. Then he said grudgingly, "I like the lass better, myself, I think." But he did not take Susan's hand or look kindly at her.

He left them and made a pot of tea, and brought it on a tray with three cups and some loaf sugar. Then he found some bread and excellent cheese, and even a jar of quince preserves, such as Mr. Pepys bought at Queen's Market. They partook silently, thoughtfully. It was a hard session.

Amos got up and walked the floor. "Mr. McTarvish," he said, "you've been more than kind to Kip and me. You've taught us some arithmetic, and you've even taught Kip to read. You've steered me on the right course a couple of times. I'm deeply obliged. But finally a man has to make his own plans. I'll use my gold guineas to get Kip and me to America on a merchant ship. That's because I don't want to indenture myself and him for four or five years of servitude. We've not got time for that. At least I've not, because I want to marry Susan. And Kip would be troublesome to any master that bought him. He and I will start life over there as free people, I hope, if we go. Then, as quick as I could take care of my mother and Susan, the houseboat could be sold to Nokes, to pay their passage."

"Very pretty, Amos," McTarvish snorted. "Very fine and bonny. But first get Kip and yourself out of England."

"I said I'd use the guineas for our passage, sir."

"See here, Amos, there's a thing or two in your way." Mr. McTarvish spoke patiently this time, for he was sorry to spoil the hopes of this sorely beset young man. "All merchantmen are searched at Gravesend for felons and deserting sailors. A master couldn't clear port if he declined the search. Kip would be apprehended as the King's Ward that fled Bridewell. You'd be an accomplice up to your neck. Kip would go to Jamaica, for all your trouble. And you'd be seized for the King's Navy, leaving your dependents stranded."

"I didn't know all this, sir," Amos said dejectedly.

"Amos," Susan spoke up, "take me to Woolwich. Take me to Barbara Sheldon. She's married to Mr. Ralph Wood, the mastmaker's son. They have some ships that go to America for masts. They're not merchantmen."

"But still subject to the laws of England, Susan," McTarvish said. "Would they evade them for you?" He raised sarcastic eyebrows. "Do you have such influence with the Wood family?"

"Barbara is my friend, Mr. McTarvish," Susan answered simply. She thanked him for the tea and fastened her coat, detesting him, yet respecting his flinty realities.

Amos and Susan walked to Wapping Stairs and took barge to Woolwich, talking lightly to keep up their courage. They counted how many Sheldons they knew of. There was the Archbishop of Canterbury in his gaiters. And Sheriff Sheldon in his necklace of office. And Captain Sheldon, an old soldier with a wooden leg, who clumped around Tower Hill. Then there were the Sheldons who kept lodgers in Woolwich, the parents of the girl they were on their way to see.

They found her with her husband, young Mr. Wood, just finishing supper at their own handsome fireside. Barbara embraced Susan and showed her approval of Amos.

"I don't wonder you want to marry him, Susan," she said, being her usual gay, kind, honest self. "I'm sure many girls do. I might myself, if I didn't have Ralph." She offered them supper, which they declined in a strangely absent-minded way.

"Is something wrong?" Barbara asked, puzzled.

"Oh, very wrong, Barbara," Susan answered. "When your servant goes out of the room, I'll tell you."

The servant left, and Barbara made sure the door was shut. "Now," she said. "I suppose Ralph can hear, too?"

"Oh, yes, Barbara! Especially him. We need his help."

"If I can lend you any money—" said young Mr. Wood, uncertain of what was expected of him. "Any friend of my wife's who happens to be hard pressed—"

"No, sir," Amos said quickly. "We didn't come to borrow money. But I'm afraid what we need is less to your liking, Mr. Wood. My brother, Kip Skeet, is in bad trouble, and they're trying to ship him to Jamaica. He's just fourteen years old. I need to take him to America on one of your ships. We'd have to go as stowaways, he and myself, till you're at sea. After that we'd be at the shipmaster's service, to work in the hold or at the rigging. We've got passage money, besides," he added with dignity. "But we'd not be coming back to England. That's the way it is."

Susan said, "And that's not the whole of it, Mr. Wood. Kip hasn't done anything evil. It only looks evil. It's really a sorry mess. Amos, tell the whole thing, from the start."

"Suppose we sit down by the fire and have some fresh cider," Mr. Wood said, and he took crystal glasses from a cabinet, and a demijohn of cider from a cool spot near a window, and made every one comfortable. He was a most likable young man, for all that he was wealthy enough to incite envy; and it was evident that he adored his wife, whom Mr. Pepys had given such a poor rating in facial beauty and social prominence.

Amos was not a good talker, being a groper for words, but he got through.

"We've got a ship going at week's end," Mr. Wood remarked, casually pouring cider again. "The last one we're sending over till spring. You and Kip are welcome to passage. I'll arrange for you both to stow below till you're at sea. A Wood ship is rarely searched, but it could happen now."

"I can't tell you how I thank you, sir," Amos said humbly. He was stunned by Mr. Ralph Wood's simple and immediate consent. And so was Susan. They had braced themselves for overcoming objections. Or for the ordeal of pleading, which would have been harder.

"We are not licensed to carry passengers," young Mr. Wood said with a grin, "so we can't take those guineas you found. Put a few in your pockets. Give the rest to Susan, to use for herself and your mother. Mr. Pepys can keep them for her in his strongbox."

He went out of the room and returned with a large map, which he proceeded to spread on the floor. "Here's the At-

lantic Ocean, both sides," he said. "It's the latest map put out by the Navy." They all went to the floor to study it.

The colony of Virginia was located easily, being so large. "Too warm and sandy near the coast," Ralph Wood said. "No hardwoods that we can get at. Now here's New England, where we get our trees. Boston, this port is called. And here's Salem. We get magnificent masts in those places. They're floated down the rivers to us, cleanly trimmed. I expect you would like New England, Skeet. Maybe you could find work in Massachusetts."

"Kip and I've got jobs waiting for us on the Delaware River," Amos explained proudly. "There's a tannery there that needs men and boys. Can you show me Delaware Bay, sir?"

"Yes. Here it is. But we don't go there. The only port our ships touch before New England is New York—that place we got from the Dutch. Our shipmasters like it best of the whole coast, and so do the sailors. My father lets them anchor in that harbor for a week or two. There's something about New York, apparently. It's on a mighty river with granite cliffs— the Hudson. They say it fairly takes your breath, for grandeur. And the town's growing by leaps and bounds."

"Our Delaware settlement is close to New York," Amos said. "Kip and I could get there by stage, I expect. Or any sort of wagon for hire."

"Then you're in luck, Skeet. And so will Susan and your mother be when they go over. Nearly all merchantmen sail for New York."

He talked then of how he intended to make the crossing in a couple of years "just to see America" if Barbara would go, too. "But hardly on one of the Wood tubs," he said, laughing.

"Oh, I'll go," Barbara declared, "even on a mast carrier. I'm dying for a voyage!" She and Mr. Wood kissed, and Susan and Amos kissed. And at Barbara's suggestion they all took hands and did a circle dance around the map on the floor. For Barbara was that kind of girl. And in the years to come, when she and her husband would go to New England about the masts, she would lighten Boston's staid gatherings with her buoyancy.

Ralph Wood went to his study and got his journal, a leather-bound book in which were entered the Wood firm's commitments.

"Our ship *Westerly* sails Friday, November ninth," he reported. "Out with the night tide. She leaves from the Wood docks at Deptford, where she's moored. Be there with your brother soon after dark, Skeet, to board her. I'll be on the dock. My father leaves the departures to me, especially in bad seasons."

Amos muttered: "Deptford. Wood docks. *Westerly*. Friday, November ninth. Board her soon after dark."

He shook hands with the Woods, repeating the words. Susan followed him, and she took up the chant, as if Amos might forget.

Going home on the barge, they thought persistently of the thing they had lost track of during their comfortable visit. Kip must be found and got to the ship. Or all this bright hope and wondrous opportunity was for nothing. This was Tuesday night. They had just three days.

Kip did not pick his first Alsatian lodging with enough care, and so suffered, mentally and physically. The house sign had attracted him. Duke and Dog, it said, and so he went in and asked for accommodations. But the sign was a misnomer. The keeper was very lowborn, and there was no dog in sight. Dining facilities were of the worst; Kip could not stomach the strange dinner of tripe, or the greasy platters at supper. The lodgers, it turned out, slept four to a room. Kip used the floor rather than share a bed with any of his repellent roommates. But at least none questioned him. All seemed sunk in their own problems too deeply to be interested in another's. Kip left after breakfast.

He chose his next abode, the Wool Sack, more for its looks than for its name. It was fairly clean, and there were no broken windows stuffed with rags. Furthermore, an impressive lodger sat on a bench outside, reading a book. He was a Jewish gentleman, wearing sedate broadcloth, a beard, and a skullcap.

On the second morning of Kip's sojourn there, he paid down another two shillings, having decided to dig in.

The Jewish gentleman had gone outside with his book. Kip followed and sat at the other end of the bench. "I hope we can be friends, sir," he said experimentally.

"Jehovah forbid," the man replied, glancing at him. Alsatia's boys were famously formidable, and Kip was as tattered as the rest of them. Bridewell had not helped his appearance.

Though rejected, Kip was not entirely discouraged. He continued to sit on the bench. He watched the passers-by. There came two women, carrying home a basket of wilted vegetables from some unsavory street market, and their progress was marked by loud laughter and drunken staggering. He thought them quite terrible, and he felt complacently thankful that his own mother had never made a spectacle of herself when in her cups, but had kept to her house and wept.

Men passed furtively. Thin children roamed aimlessly. Five or six boys approached in compact formation. They spied him; paused; motioned with strange jerks of the head for him to get up and join them.

"I can't," Kip said. "I'm with my uncle here."

They went their way, and the Jewish gentleman eyed Kip with amusement. "An ugly crew," he commented.

"Yes, sir. Hardly my kind."

"What is your kind, may I ask?"

Kip told a good deal about himself, for he was like his mother in his need to communicate. Not that he had forgotten the guard's warning against chumming; he remembered it, but he instinctively trusted this quiet, remote man.

"A thought-provoking story," the listener said, holding his place in his book. "Justice miscarried."

"And why are *you* here, sir?"

"It's very simple. I'm hiding from my creditors." Seeing

Kip's expectant look, he continued. "I broke when my ship was lost. It was not insured. Some of the investors have judgments against me. I'm due for Bridewell. If I can get to France, I can get credit and start again. I can pay off my debts. But not in Bridewell."

"How long have you been in Whitefriars, sir?"

"Two months. I'm waiting for a friend."

"The way I'm waiting for my brother."

"Even so." He resumed his reading.

Getting no more conversation, Kip went exploring in the main ways of Whitefriars, wisely keeping out of blind alleys and courts. Returning, he felt compelled to interrupt the reading Jew.

"What's that place just over the tall wall, sir?"

"It's Inner Temple. Beyond is Middle Temple. They are the great law colleges."

"Do you know something, sir, there's a wicket gate in the big gate, and a person could open it if he tried."

The reader sighed. "I sometimes do, myself," he said, "but never in the daytime. I visit the gardens." He resumed reading.

Kip went away, toward the gate.

A while later the Jewish gentleman was interrupted again. "Let me intrude," a harsh Scotch voice said. "I'm looking for a boy," and he described Kip accurately. "Do you know such a one?"

The reader inspected the speaker with disfavor. McTarvish was wearing a leather cap and hunting coat and he had a beagle dog on a long leash. The dog was almost unmanageable, whining and testing the bench and earth with nervous sniffs. "I think the lad I'm looking for must be somewhere about," McTarvish insisted.

"Whitefriars has its quota of boys. I can't notice all of them."

"But this is desperate. The lad's wanted."

"I'm hardly an informer. None in Alsatia is."

"You don't understand, sir. The lad's in trouble with the

City and must be got out of London. He can have protection if he'll come with me. He knows me, I assure you, and he knows the dog."

"He said his brother would come."

"Ah! So you do know the lad! You've talked with him!"

"I admit nothing. State your case."

McTarvish did so. He was compelled to tell of the ship at Deptford, and of the need of haste.

"Go through the wicket in the gate in Temple wall. I think you'll find him. If you fail, he's staying at this inn."

"God bless you, sir," McTarvish said, and made haste away, the beagle pulling ahead.

Kip was wandering over the quiet pavements of Middle Temple when McTarvish and Singer espied him. The meeting between boy and dog might have been noisy if McTarvish had not muted it by gesturing caution and shortening Singer's leash.

"Take your dog and go down Temple Stairs toward the river," he said, "but in a tarrying way. Inspect the gardens from the pavements. Don't let your hound at the shrubs. I must go for Amos. I left him in a tobacco shop in Salisbury Court."

"Let me and Singer go with you, Mr. McTarvish," Kip begged; for waiting had not so much worn him down as it had keyed him up.

"Do as I tell you, Kip."

McTarvish found Amos at the front of the shop where he had left him. Amos saw that the dog was lacking. "Does it mean—?" He could not get the words out. He looked so spent and gaunt that McTarvish pitied him anew.

"Yes. Kip's got Singer. In a way, the dog found him. Though there was help from an educated Jew. I wish I had seen what he was reading," McTarvish added regretfully.

"Was Kip reading?" Amos asked dazedly.

"No, no. The man on the bench. Very cultivated. Very composed. I nae ken such composure under stress."

"Where now, Mr. McTarvish?"

"I sent Kip to Temple Stairs. We're all going to cross the river there and take a country road into Surrey. Deptford, you'll remember, even though you're past thinking, is on Surrey side of Thames. We'll hunt rabbits today. At dusk we'll move in back of Deptford, avoiding the King's Yards like the plague. We'll find the Wood docks as best we can. I must buy a fowling piece now. My wife's parsimony kept me using a poor one all my married life."

He bought a very good hunting rod in a shop that boasted: GUN MAKERS TO THE EARLS OF BEDFORD; and the sign was no doubt accurate, as the Russell town house was fairly close, in the Strand. McTarvish reveled in his extravagance. "How fine and braw," he exclaimed, "to buy the kind of gun a wife would object to!"

They went into Fleet Street and through Temple Bar, and walked toward Temple Stairs. "No to-do, mind you, when you meet your brother," McTarvish warned. So Amos said, "Well, there, Kip. How goes it?" and smoothed the boy's rumpled hair, to make it less noticeably neglected, and pretended that neither of them had tears in their eyes. "I'm wearing two coats," he said. "One's for you. You can put it on in Southwark."

They crossed to Southwark; and from there took a country road into Surrey, as planned. Singer flushed some rabbits, as if to prove his lineage, but McTarvish neglected to fire. "Some other day," he said lamely. Actually, he was shaking, and his stomach hurt fiercely.

At dusk they approached Deptford—the town itself, which lay downstream from the King's Yards. They walked through the crowded streets to the river, and had no difficulty finding the Wood docks. A ship was there, large and ugly and stanch and battered. Her mainmast was magnificent, probably the best ever cut in Massachusetts. In the twilight her name could still be discerned: *Westerly*.

McTarvish left Amos and Kip beside some cargo and went

onto the dock, where young Mr. Wood was standing, rigid and alert.

"The lads are here, Mr. Ralph," McTarvish whispered. "Is it too early?"

"Too early? No! I thought they'd missed. We've been searched. Call them. I'll take them aboard."

And he did, dog and all.

McTarvish immediately went upriver by barge and got off at Tower Stairs. He hurried to Seething Lane and reported to Susan, who had all but collapsed with anxiety because of Kip's not having been found. At his news, she laughed and wept in relief, and asked him to tell it all twice. They parted as friends, she having praised his new gun and given him some rennet for his stomach, he having assured her he no longer, *under certain circumstances*, objected to early marriages.

"I doubt you'll be a nuisance to Amos in any way," he conceded. "It occurs to me you'll teach him to read and write. I'd like some letters from Amos, through the years."

"Dear, kind Mr. McTarvish!" she said. "I'll see that Amos writes to you when I'm his wife."

A bit later, after nine o'clock, London had another fire. Flames lit the western sky. "This would be monotonous," Pepys called out to Admiral Penn from his attic window, "if it weren't so frightening!" News had come that Whitehall Palace was afire, having caught from burning straw in the Horse Guards' tilt yard. As Pepys reported it in his journal before retiring:

And so we run up to the garret, and find it so; a horrid great fire; and by and by we saw and heard part of it blown up with powder. The ladies began presently to be afeard: one fell in fits. [Pegg Penn, who was excitable.] *The whole town in an alarm. Drums and trumpets, and the Horse-guards everywhere spread, running up and down in the street. And I began to have mighty apprehensions how things might be, for we are in expectation, from common gossip, this night, or tomorrow, to have an invasion and massacre. . . . By and by comes news that the fire has slackened; so that we were a little cheered up again* [they were having a party], *and to supper, pretty merry.*

When Pepys went to the kitchen to speed the supper service, Susan Stokes eyed him triumphantly. Her cheeks were red, and she had a sparkling look. "Let them lay *that* fire to Kip Skeet!" she said. "Let them try!"

"Do you mean they can't?" Pepys asked with relief; for if he had guessed right on young Skeet, he would forevermore sleep better.

"Kip was far away from the scene of the crime this time, Mr. Pepys," Susan told him. "Today Amos and Kip and Mr. McTarvish—the Lime House man—went rabbit hunting in Surrey. It seemed a good thing to do. About dusk the two boys went aboard the Wood ship *Westerly* at Deptford. They're bound for America."

"Mighty comfortable to hear," Pepys said. "Mighty! And will you be finding another sweetheart, Susan?"

"No, I'm keeping the same old one, Mr. Pepys, but you'll be finding a new cook's helper. I'm going to join Amos in America next summer."

"Then let me salute you tonight," he said. "There's no time like November."

Laughing, Susan successfully dodged the inevitable Pepys kiss, probably the only pretty maidservant in that house who ever had.